My Congratulations to the
"Presents" Series and to its
Readers —
May the Romance live on!

With my very best wishes
Penny Jordan

Welcome to Penny Jordan's miniseries featuring the Crighton family.

This is no ordinary family because, although the Crightons might appear to have it all, shocking revelations and heartache lie just beneath the surface of their perfect, charmed lives.

When a young woman comes in search of her inheritance, further family secrets and scandals are exposed.

Penny Jordan has been writing for more than fifteen years and has an outstanding record: over 100 novels published, including the phenomenally successful *Power Games*, *Cruel Legacy* and *Power Play*, which hit the *New York Times* and *Sunday Times* bestseller lists.

Her latest mainstream release—*A Perfect Family*—gives the full inside story of the Crighton family and is available through MIRA® Books. Their story continues in three Harlequin Presents® novels:

The Perfect Seduction (#1941 March 1998)

Perfect Marriage Material (#1948 April 1998)

The Perfect Match? (#1954 May 1998)

Look out in 1999 for further passion and drama in the Crighton household.

Penny Jordan

The Perfect Match?

Harlequin Books

TORONTO • NEW YORK • LONDON
AMSTERDAM • PARIS • SYDNEY • HAMBURG
STOCKHOLM • ATHENS • TOKYO • MILAN
MADRID • WARSAW • BUDAPEST • AUCKLAND

ISBN 0-373-11954-2

THE PERFECT MATCH?

First North American Publication 1998.

Printed in U.S.A.

The Crighton Family

BEN CRIGHTON: Proud patriarch of the family, a strong-minded character in his seventies, determined to see his dynasty thrive and prosper.

RUTH REYNOLDS: Ben's sister, a vibrant woman now happily reunited with Grant, the man from whom she was tragically separated during the war years—and also with the daughter she gave up for adoption. Ruth is a caring, perceptive woman and she holds the Crighton family together.

JON AND JENNY CRIGHTON: Steady, family-oriented couple. Jon keeps the Crighton law firm running smoothly, and Jenny is a partner in a local antiques business with Guy Cooke. Guy helped Jenny through difficult times in her marriage. He has always been close to Jenny, and they have a strong friendship.

MAX CRIGHTON: Son of Jon and Jenny, a self-assured, sexy, ruthlessly ambitious lawyer who married his wife, Madeleine, a gentle woman and daughter of a High Court judge, to advance his career. The couple lives in London with their two children, but Madeleine has concerns about the stability of their marriage....

ROSE OLDHAM: Rose had connections with the Crighton family when she was growing up—as did her mother and grandmother. But she's since moved away from the area and is reluctant to return to Haslewich when her brother dies, sending her daughter Chrissie instead.

CHRISSIE OLDHAM: Rose's daughter, a spirited but romantic English teacher who is convinced her ideal hero just doesn't exist. She longs for a passionate, unconventional man—and is astonished when she arrives in Haslewich to be swept off her feet by the broodingly sensual Guy Cooke....

GUY COOKE: Jenny's partner in a successful antiques business, Guy is close to the Crighton family and very loyal to Jenny. He has Gypsy ancestors and is devastatingly sexy and adored by women. Fiery and impetuous, he's the exact opposite of gentle Chrissie—but feels an instant bond when he meets her.

The Crighton Family

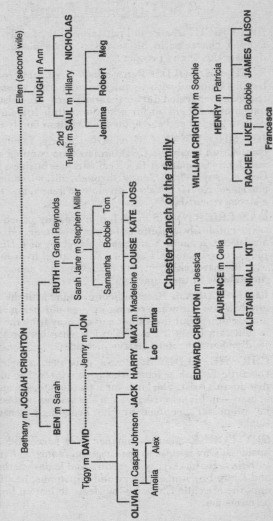

Haslewich branch of the family

- .... m Ellen (second wife)
  - HUGH m Ann
    - NICHOLAS
    - 2nd Tullah m SAUL m Hillary
      - Jemima
      - Robert
      - Meg
- Bethany m JOSIAH CRIGHTON ....
  - BEN m Sarah
    - RUTH m Grant Reynolds
      - Sarah Jane m Stephen Miller
        - Samantha
        - Bobbie
        - Tom
    - Jenny m JON
      - MAX m Madeleine LOUISE KATE JOSS
      - JACK HARRY
      - Leo Emma
  - Tiggy m DAVID
    - OLIVIA m Caspar Johnson
      - Amelia
      - Alex

Chester branch of the family

- EDWARD CRIGHTON m Jessica
  - LAURENCE m Celia
    - ALISTAIR NIALL KIT
- WILLIAM CRIGHTON m Sophie
  - HENRY m Patricia
    - RACHEL LUKE m Bobbie JAMES ALISON
      - Francesca

CHAPTER ONE

'AND you're sure you don't mind going to Haslewich to sort out everything...?'

'No, Mum, I don't mind at all,' Chrissie assured her mother quietly, exchanging looks over her head with her father as she did so.

It was no secret in their small, close-knit family unit just how much her younger brother's irresponsible behaviour and alcoholic lifestyle had upset Chrissie's mother.

In the early years of her marriage she had tried her best to help Charles, naïvely believing that he was genuinely trying to mend his ways. But eight years ago, following a short custodial sentence after he had been convicted of stealing several small items from the home of an acquaintance, which he had later sold to pay for the drink on which he was by then dependent, Chrissie's mother had decided that enough was enough and had cut herself off from him completely.

Chrissie understood just why she had felt compelled to do so.

Her father was a hard-working heart surgeon in a busy local hospital in the small Scottish border town where they lived and her mother was a member of the local town council and involved in several local charities.

Her brother's unsavoury reputation and dishonest

behaviour was so completely opposite to her own way of life that it was very hard for her to deal with the situation.

Now though, Uncle Charles was dead and someone, *one* of them, would have to travel to Cheshire to sort things out, dispose of the small property he had owned in the centre of the town of Haslewich—all that was left from his share of the farmhouse and land that he and Chrissie's mother had inherited from their parents, and Chrissie had volunteered to take on the task.

'Heaven knows what kind of state the house will be in.' Chrissie's mother gave a small shudder. 'The last time I was there the whole place was filthy and you couldn't open a single cupboard door without an empty bottle falling out.

'I just wish I knew why he…' She closed her eyes. 'Even as a child he was different…awkward…self-destructive, very different from our father. He was such a kind, gentle man like my grandfather, but Charles… We were never very close as children, perhaps because of the big age gap between us.' She shook her head.

'I feel guilty about letting you go down to Haslewich on your own but we've got this conference in Mexico followed by your father's lecture tour.'

'Look, Mum, it's all right,' Chrissie reiterated. 'I don't mind, honestly, and it isn't as though I don't have the time.'

There was a big reshuffle going on in the English department of the school where Chrissie worked as a teacher and she had already warned her parents she had heard on the grapevine that the department was looking to cut costs and shed some staff.

'Well, I'm not entirely happy about your having to stay in Charles's house,' her mother told her.

'But that *is* the whole point of my going,' Chrissie reminded her wryly. 'The house has to be sold to help pay off Uncle Charles's debts and you said yourself that there was no way it could be put on the market until it had been cleaned from top to bottom.'

'I know. Which reminds me, I'll have to get in touch with the bank and the solicitors to make sure you've got my authority to deal with all the necessary paperwork.'

Once again Chrissie and her father shared a look over her mother's head.

Charles Platt had not just left behind him an untidy house and an unsavoury reputation; there was also a large number of outstanding debts.

In truth, she wasn't particularly looking forward to being the one to sort out the mess Uncle Charles had left behind, Chrissie admitted, but someone had to do it and she certainly wasn't going to let her mother be even more upset than she was already by letting her see her own distaste for the task.

The last time she had visited Haslewich had been following her grandmother's death, and her memories of the occasion and the area were coloured by her mother's grief.

Her Uncle Charles had been living with his mother in the old Cheshire farmhouse that had been passed down through many generations of their family, but her grandfather, disappointed in his son and well aware of his weakness, had sold off the land to another farmer, and following his wife's death the farm-house itself had been sold, as well.

She could still remember the searing shame she had felt on seeing her Uncle Charles staggering from one of the town's many public houses whilst she had been shopping there with her mother. When a group of children had jeered at him and mocked him, her mother had drawn a quick, sharp breath and gone white before turning round and abruptly walking Chrissie off in the opposite direction.

That had been the first time she had become aware of the reason for the pain in her mother's face and voice whenever she mentioned her brother.

Now, as an adult, Chrissie was, of course, fully *au fait* with the history of her uncle's addiction to alcohol and gambling.

Weak and vain, he was something of a misfit in the local farming community in which he had grown up, and it had been obvious even before he reached his teens that he was not going to follow in the family tradition of farming.

'He broke my father's heart,' Chrissie's mother had once told her sadly. 'Dad did his best, selling off small pieces of land so that he could give Charles an allowance. He tried to understand and support him when he said that he wanted to be an actor. But it was all just an excuse to get money out of Dad and spend his time gambling and drinking, initially in Chester and then, when his cronies there got wise to him, back in Haslewich.'

And as they had talked, Chrissie had recognised how hurt her grandparents and her mother had been by her uncle's behaviour, how his attitudes to life, which were so very different from theirs, confused them. How impossible they found it to understand how he could so easily and carelessly flout the moral laws they lived their lives by and, most painful of all perhaps, how shamed they felt by him.

And now he was dead and with him had died a small piece of Haslewich history. Platts had farmed the land around Haslewich for over three centuries as the headstones on their graves in Haslewich's churchyard testified, but no longer.

'Don't get upset,' Chrissie urged her mother, going over to put her arm round her and kiss her.

Facially they were very similar, with wide-set, almond-shaped eyes and high cheek-bones in a delicately feminine face, but where her mother was small, barely five foot two and softly rounded, Chrissie had inherited her father's height and leaner body frame.

She also had, quite mysteriously since both her parents were dark-haired, hair the colour of richly polished chestnuts, thick and straight and healthily glossy.

At twenty-seven going on twenty-eight, she considered herself mature enough to be above being flattered by those men who did a double take when they saw her for the first time, plainly expecting her to feel complimented by their admiration of her face and body without having bothered to take the time to learn anything about her, the person. Physical attractiveness was not, in her opinion, the prime factor in motivating a new relationship. For her there had to be something far more compelling than that. For her there had to be a sense of being instinctively drawn to the other person, 'knowing' that the magnetic pull between the two of them was too overwhelming, too powerful, to be ignored. She was, in short, a true romantic, although she was very loath to admit it.

'It's not fair,' one of her friends had told her mock-crossly the previous summer.

'If I had your looks I know I'd make much better use of them than you do. You don't *know* how lucky you are.'

'True beauty comes from within,' Chrissie had told her gently—and meant it.

Whilst she had been at university, she had been approached by a talent scout for a modelling agency but had refused to take them seriously.

There were those who had wondered if her irrepressible sense of humour was quite the thing one wanted in a schoolteacher, but Chrissie had proved that the ability to see and laugh at the humorous side of life was no bar to being able to teach—and to teach well.

'I'm still not entirely happy about the idea of your staying in Charles's house,' her mother repeated.

Chrissie sat down opposite her.

'Mum...we've already been through all this,' she reminded her. 'The whole point of my going to Haslewich is to prepare the house for sale and the best way I can do that is if I'm living there.'

'Yes, you're right, of course. But knowing how Charles lived...' Her mother gave a small shudder.

She was a meticulous housewife, a wonderful cook, the true daughter of ancestors who had spent their lives scrubbing dairies and stone floors, polishing, washing and waging war on dirt in all its many forms.

'I've got my own bedding and my own towels and utensils,' Chrissie reminded her mother.

'I should be doing this,' Rose Oldham protested. 'Charles is…was my brother….'

'And *my* uncle,' Chrissie pointed out, adding, 'And besides, you can't. You don't have the time right now and I do.'

Although she wasn't going to say as much to her mother who she knew, despite her modern outlook on life, was still eagerly waiting for the day when Chrissie became a wife and mother, she had been rather glad of the excuse of having to go to Haslewich. It had enabled her to turn down an invitation from a fellow teacher who had been pursuing her all term to join him and a group of friends in Provence for the summer.

Provence had been very tempting, but the teacher had not. Privately, Chrissie had always been a little wary of her weakness for men of a distinctly swash-buckling and impetuous nature and more suited to the pages of an historical romance than modern-day society and it was one she very firmly squashed whenever she felt it stirring.

The fellow teacher had not come anywhere near creating any kind of stir within her and would, no doubt, have made excellent husband and father material, but he certainly wouldn't have done anything to satisfy that quirky and rather regrettable feminine desire she knew she had for a man who would excite and entice her, a man who would challenge her, match her, a man with a capital *M*.

Well, one thing was for sure, she certainly wasn't

likely to find him in Haslewich, which by all her reck-
oning was a sleepy little market town, a quiet back-
water where nothing much ever happened.

CHAPTER TWO

'I TAKE it they still haven't caught whoever broke into Queensmead?' Guy Cooke asked Jenny Crighton as she came into the small antiques shop in which they were co-partners.

'No,' Jenny told him, shaking her head as she responded to his enquiry about the recent theft and break-in at her father-in-law's home.

She smiled warmly at Guy as she spoke. He really was the most extraordinarily good-looking man and if she wasn't so firmly and happily married to her own husband she had to admit that it could have been all too easy to join the long queue of women who sighed dreamily over Guy's very masculine blend of a virilely powerful and tautly muscled male body—the kind of body that would have allowed him to pose for a trendily provocative jeans advert any day of the week—allied to enigmatically hooded eyes set above high cheek-bones and a certain way of looking at you that was completely irresistible, virtually resulting in a complete meltdown. Add to that highly sensual cocktail the intensely masculine genes he had inherited from his Gypsy forebears and the reputation that went with them and it was easy to understand why the word 'sexy' accompanied by a longing look was the way most of her sex would quite freely have described him.

Not that Jenny was totally immune to Guy's looks

or the unexpected and even more dangerous generosity and warmth of character that went with them, but she loved Jon and she thought it was very sad that with all he had to offer a woman, Guy had not yet found the right one for him.

'At least they didn't harm Ben,' she added. 'But it has shaken him. You know how stubborn he can be normally and how hard Jon and I have found it to try to persuade him to have someone to live in.'

'Tell me about it,' Guy invited. 'When I went up there to do a valuation on the antiques for his insurance company, he practically hit the roof when I told him that he was going to need to have an alarm system installed. I take it he never did?'

'Well, you know Ben,' Jenny sighed. 'Luckily they didn't take very much and the police think they must have been disturbed either by the phone ringing or by someone arriving at the house.'

'It's so hard to contemplate that someone would actually break in in broad daylight and calmly proceed to remove not just small items but actual pieces of furniture, as well.'

'The police did warn us that there's very little chance of our getting anything back. Apparently there's been a spate of these kinds of robberies recently and they think it's gangs coming out from the city wanting to make money to buy drugs. The new motorways, of course, facilitate a quick getaway and make them and the stolen property so much harder to trace.'

'But you've managed to persuade the old boy to have someone living in?' Guy questioned her as he started to check through the contents of a large packing case that contained goods from a house clearance. Junk in the main, he suspected, but you never knew....

'Well, unfortunately, no,' Jenny replied. 'But Maddy is due to arrive at the end of the week. You know she always comes up from London to spend a few weeks here in the summer.'

'Will Max be coming with her?' Guy asked, referring to Jon and Jenny's elder son and Maddy's husband.

Jenny bit her lip. 'No…no, he won't. It seems he's heavily involved on a case at the moment and he's going to have to fly out to Spain to see his client. She's got a yacht that's apparently in a marina out there.'

Max was a barrister working from a prestigious set of chambers in London. He specialised in divorce work and it hadn't escaped Guy's notice that most of his clients were women. Max liked women, or rather he liked the boost to his ego that deceiving them gave him.

Guy did not have a very high opinion of Max but he cared far too much for Jenny to let her know it.

Life hadn't always been easy for Jenny and although she and her husband, Jon, were happy together now…

Unlike Max, Guy genuinely did like women, all women, but some women especially so. Women like Jenny—warm, gentle, womanly women with quiet, understated beauty. Their more flashy, visually eye-catching counterparts held very little allure for Guy. He was a physically good-looking man himself and well knew how worthless mere good looks could be. A warm, loving, caring nature, though, now *that* was something that time could never erode, something enduring and worthy of loving, cherishing…

But he had long ago come to accept that Jenny was not for him; that she loved her husband and would never see him as anything more than a friend. 'A much younger friend' as she had once stressed to him, reminding him of the age gap between them. At thirty-nine Guy no longer considered himself to be particularly 'young'.

'Apart from the shock of the burglary itself, the thing that's upset Ben the most,' Jenny was saying, 'is losing the little yew desk. His father apparently had it copied from the French original that belonged to *his* grandmother. It was a very pretty little piece, but being a copy, not really of any great financial value.'

'But a good deal of sentimental value,' Guy suggested.

'Very much so,' Jenny concurred. 'When I was talking to Luke about it the other day, he told me that the Chester side of the family owned a matching pair of the original from which Ben's desk was copied and that they had been gifts brought back from France for the twin daughters of the Crighton who bought them. His father now has one of them and his uncle the other.'

'Mmm…well, perhaps the thief or thieves didn't realise Ben's was a copy.'

'Maybe not, although the police seem to think they probably took it because it was in the hallway and easy to move like the silver and jewellery they took.

'Ruth and I had to spend virtually a whole day checking over the house and listing what was missing.

Ben certainly wasn't in any fit state to help and although, of course, I had some knowledge of what should have been there, Ruth, as Ben's sister, was naturally much more accurate.'

'She's back from the States, then?'

'Yes, she and Grant flew in on Saturday.' Jenny laughed. 'I think it's wonderful how the two of them have stuck to their agreement to spend alternate three months in one another's countries.'

'It's lovely to see them together. They're so much in love, even now.'

'Well, I imagine all that they've been through must make the time they're having together now all the more precious.'

'I agree. Real confirmation that fact can be stranger than fiction.'

'And real love so strong that nothing can diminish or destroy it,' Jenny added softly. 'In all the years they were apart, neither of them was ever tempted to marry someone else.'

'But at least they're together now and so deeply in love that Bobbie complains that despite the fact that they were all married at the same time, Ruth and Grant are a far more romantic couple than her and Luke.'

'Well, Bobbie and Luke do have a young child and two busy careers,' Guy commented, 'while her grandparents are both retired and free to concentrate exclusively on one another.'

'They may both be retired but Ruth is still on half a dozen local committees as well as running her single-parent units,' Jenny reminded him. 'And Grant has an extraordinary spread of business interests to

keep him busy. I sometimes feel exhausted just listening to what they've been doing. I can't help com-
paring their energy and the enjoyment they get out of
life with Ben's growing lack of interest in everything.'

Jenny's forehead pleated in a worried frown as she
reflected on her father-in-law.

'Is he still going ahead with his hip-joint replace-
ment operation?' Guy asked her.

'I hope so,' Jenny told him feelingly. 'It's sched-
uled for the end of the summer and the plan was that
Maddy would be there when he comes out of hospital
to look after him. He responds far better to her than
he does to any of us, partially because she's Max's
wife, of course, and so far as Ben is concerned, Max
can do no wrong.'

'But not so far as you, Max's mother, are concerned,' Guy offered shrewdly.

Jenny shook her head. 'Ben has always spoiled
Max and Max has never needed any encouragement
to believe he deserves to receive preferential treatment. I did hope that when he and Maddy married…'
She stopped and shook her head, changing the subject
to ask, 'Anything interesting in that lot?'

'Not really,' Guy replied, taking his cue from her
and letting the subject drop, switching from discussing personal matters to their shared business interests.
'I've had a call to do another house clearance this
morning although I doubt that there'll be anything
there of any interest. Charlie Platt,' he added grimly.

'Charlie Platt?' Jenny queried, frowning again, then
her expression clearing. 'Oh yes, I know who you
mean.'

'Yes,' Guy went on. 'By all accounts he virtually drank himself to death.'

'Oh, poor man,' Jenny sympathised compassionately.

'Poor man nothing,' Guy told her grimly. 'He was the biggest con man in town. His parents publicly disowned him. He died leaving debts all over the place.'

From the tone of his voice, Jenny wondered if Guy was one of the people he had owed money to. If so, she doubted that Guy would admit, even to her, that he had been taken advantage of.

Normally an easygoing, compassionate man, generally inclined to judge others gently rather than harshly, he also possessed a surprisingly fierce streak of pride, accentuated, Jenny suspected, by the fact that his family, the Cooke clan, various members of whom were spread throughout the town, had originated, so local history had it, from the unsanctified union of one of a band of travelling Romany Gypsies and the naïvely innocent daughter of a town schoolmaster. They were generally held in a mixture of awe and contempt by their less enterprising and energetic peers.

The girl had been married off in haste and disgrace to a local widowed tavern keeper desperately in need of someone to take charge of his sprawling brood of existing children.

Dependent upon where you stood in the local hierarchy, there was a tendency to regard the activities of the Cooke clan, both professionally and privately, as extremely suspect or extremely enviable.

Over the generations, the name Cooke had become synonymous, not just with the local taverns and public houses that they ran, but also with such disparate activities as poaching, gaming and other enterprising methods of increasing their income, a habit the more God-fearing local folk were inclined to put down to the genes they had inherited from their roving-eyed Gypsy forebears.

Not that any members of the family went in for poaching or its equivalent these days. *That* practice had died out with his grandfather's generation, Guy had once wryly told Jenny, along with the bulk of his then-adult male relatives, most of whom had been with the Cheshire Regiment during the First World War.

'But that kind of reputation is hard to lose,' Guy had told Jenny. 'Once a Cooke, always a Cooke!'

'And having those brigandish dark good looks of yours doesn't help,' Jenny had teased him gently.

'No,' Guy had agreed shortly. He had lost count of the number of fathers who had sternly admonished their daughters against dating him when he had been younger. He thought now that he must have been the only teenage boy in the locality to have gained the reputation of being wild and dangerous whilst still possessing his virginity.

It was half-day closing, and after Jenny had left and Guy had locked up the shop, he went home to work on his other business interests, which ranged from a half share in the very popular local restaurant owned by one of his sisters and her husband to a smaller share in a firm of local builders owned by yet another relative.

He had recently been considering the validity of investing in small local properties that could be ren-ovated and then let out on short-term leases to em-

ployees of one of the large multinationals that had
recently started to move into the area.

Antiques, especially furniture, were his first love
but the business he shared with Jenny was hardly sufficient to keep him fully occupied.

He frowned as he studied the post. He and Jenny
were the prime motivators behind the Antiques Fair
that was due to be held at Fitzburgh Place the following month, a combined event to promote the area and
hopefully raise money for Jenny and Ruth's pet charity, the single mothers homes scheme, which Ruth had
started as a result of her own experiences as an unmarried mother.

As Guy started to check off the list of exhibitors to
the fair against the list of invitation letters he had sent
out, he remembered what Jenny had said about
Charlie Platt.

He and Charlie had been at school together...just.
Guy had entered the school just as Charlie was on the
verge of leaving it to move up to the seniors.

A thin, pale boy, who had suffered badly from
childhood asthma, which thankfully he had later out-
grown, Guy had shown no signs then of the fact that
as an adult male he would grow up to be strong and
muscular. He had been small and vulnerable-looking,
the youngest of his mother's brood, a quiet, studious
boy whom his female siblings had mothered and
whom Charlie Platt had immediately and instinctively
focused on as an ideal victim for his practice of black-
mailing the vulnerable into parting with their dinner
money.

Guy had tried to resist, refusing trenchantly to hand
over the money—he was, after all, well used to being

cuffed and teased by his much larger and **far** more boisterous male cousins—but he had had one fear he kept hidden from his family and that was of water. Because of his asthma, he had never been allowed to learn to swim or to play in the river that bounded the town in case the cold water brought on an attack.

Charlie Platt had very quickly discovered Guy's fear, both of the river and, even more importantly, of other people's discovering how he felt. Predictably he had made use of it.

Guy knew he would never forget the day Charlie Platt had held him under the water for so long that Guy had really believed he was going to die, probably would have died if one of his bigger and older cousins hadn't happened to come along, seen what was happening and treated Charlie Platt to the kind of rough justice that boys of that age could mete out to one another, blacking his eye, bruising his pride and putting an end to Guy's torment.

That summer, Guy had taught himself to swim, and after Charlie had left the school Guy hadn't come across him again until they were both adults, by which time Charlie was already drinking heavily and gaining something of an unsavoury reputation for himself.

And now Charlie was dead. Guy couldn't feel surprised, nor sorry, and he certainly had no desire to accommodate the terse telephone instructions he had received via his answerphone from the young woman who had announced herself as Chrissie Oldham.

Who exactly was she? She had sounded too crisp and businesslike to be one of the steady stream of women who, at one time or another, had shared

Charlie's roof. She must have been employed to sort out the estate.

Guy's frown deepened. One thing Charlie's death had done was to focus his own mind on the fact that he was close to forty with little to show for his life other than a healthy bank balance and a small group of friends.

Avril, his next to eldest sister, had complained to him at Christmas that it was high time he got married and produced a family of his own, as she watched him playing with her own grandchildren. Grandchildren!! But then Avril *was* fifteen years his senior.

He had no plans to follow her advice, though. There was no way he could share his life, commit his life…his self to another person without loving her to the point where life without her would quite simply be an untenable option.

And he had only once come even close to feeling like that and she… He got up and walked across to the window, then stood staring out at the view in front of him.

He had moved to his present house six months earlier. In a prestigious part of town, it was one in a small close of similar properties originally built to house local members of the clergy. Ruth, Jenny's aunt-in-law, lived there, three doors down; several high-ranking executives from the town's largest corporate employer, Aarlston-Becker, owned adjacent properties.

There were those who, Guy suspected even now, felt that such a house was far too grand, far too good, for a mere Cooke, even one like himself who had gone from grammar school to university and from there to all the art capitals of Europe before returning home to set up in business.

He glanced at his watch. He still had another hour before he needed to leave for Charlie Platt's house, but he had a good two hours' worth of paperwork on his desk in front of him, he reminded himself sternly.

Chrissie groaned as she straightened up and her aching back muscles protested. She had spent virtually the whole of her time since arriving in Haslewich cleaning her late uncle's small house, a task she could only relate, in terms of stress levels, to the mythical job of cleansing the Augean stables.

Every racing paper that Charlie had bought during his tenure in the house—and there had been many of them—instead of being thrown away had simply been tossed in an untidy pile on the spare-bedroom floor. This was the very room that Chrissie had planned to occupy during her hopefully brief stay. And that was just for starters. Letters, bills, in the main unpaid, junk mail, you name it—Uncle Charles had kept it.

Chrissie suspected they must have grave doubts about her at the local supermarket when she had very nearly cleaned them out of their supply of rolls of black plastic refuse sacks.

Her initial idea had been to burn the waste paper on a bonfire in the terraced cottage's small back garden, but she had soon recognised that there was far too much of it for such easy disposal and instead she had been forced to apply to the local authority for their advice and assistance on its disposal.

This morning, a couple of friendly workmen plus

an open lorry had arrived in the street to remove the sacks of paper she had prepared for them.

The cottage was one of a terrace of similar properties built into what had originally been one of the town's boundary walls using, Chrissie suspected, stone 'reclaimed' from the walls themselves and the castle, which had been virtually destroyed during the Civil War.

It could, she admitted judiciously, with a little imagination and an awful lot of determined hard work, be turned into a very attractive home for a single person or a young childless couple.

Several of the other cottages in the street had already undergone or were undergoing this process and the shiny brightness of their painted front doors highlighted the air of shabby neglect that hallmarked her uncle's cottage.

Now that she had emptied the small second bedroom, she did at least have somewhere to sleep. Her mother would have been grimly approving, no doubt, had she seen the fervour with which she had scrubbed and sanitized both the bathroom and kitchen before allowing herself to use them. She still had her reservations, though, about the wisdom of using the ancient fridge, which had formerly been home to various, thankfully unidentifiable, mouldy pieces of food.

But the worst ordeal of her visit still lay ahead of her and that was her appointment tomorrow with her late uncle's solicitors.

His clothes she had already consigned to another much smaller collection of plastic liners ready for collection by a representative of a local charity.

The house had, as she and her parents had already

guessed, revealed no material assets likely to provide enough money to help to settle his debts, with the exception of a rather attractive small yew desk.

When Chrissie had mentioned this item to her mother, she had said instantly that the desk had originally belonged to her grandmother, Chrissie's great grandmother.

'Don't arrange for it to be sold, Chrissie,' she had begged her daughter. 'We'll have it valued instead and I'll buy it from the estate. I asked Charles what had happened to it after Mother died and he said he didn't know.' She had given a small sigh. 'I suppose I ought to have guessed that he'd keep it for himself. I'm just glad that he didn't actually sell it. I suppose it's too much to hope that he kept Nan's Staffordshire figures, as well?'

'I'm sorry, Mum, but they're definitely not here,' Chrissie had told her, promising that she would have the desk appraised independently as well as by the dealer she had arranged to come and value the small, and she suspected, mainly worthless bits and pieces she had found round the house.

The desk certainly was a very attractive piece, all the more so now that she had cleaned and polished it; sturdily made it was, at the same time, very prettily feminine.

Chrissie glanced at her watch. The dealer she had been recommended to contact by her late uncle's solicitors would be here any minute. Once he had checked over and removed the bits and pieces she had placed on one side along with all the cottage's furniture—apart from the desk that was in the front room—she could arrange for the estate agent to view the cottage and put it on the market.

Tiredly she stretched her body but at least she had the satisfaction of knowing that every single nook and cranny of the small house was now clean. She still had the remnants of some of the cobwebs on her person to prove it, she acknowledged ruefully as she caught sight of the small grubby mark on her once pristine white T-shirt.

CHAPTER THREE

GUY knocked briefly on the cottage door and then waited. Knowing the way Charlie Platt had lived, he had deliberately changed into a pair of faded, well-worn jeans and an equally faded and now rather close-fitting T-shirt. The days when he had been considered an undersized weakling were now long past. It had caused him a certain amount of wry amusement when he attended antique fairs to be mistaken for one of the helpers brought in to carry the heavier pieces of furniture.

Chrissie heard the knock on the door and went to open it. Guy started to glance at her with brief disinterest, preparatory to introducing himself, and then looked at her again whilst Chrissie returned his look with the same shocked intensity.

She had heard, of course—who hadn't?—of 'love at first sight' but had always wryly dismissed it as a fairy-tale fantasy.

Surely no one in these modern times could possibly be stricken so instantly, so totally, in the space of less than a minute, or know immediately that *this* was the one, the *only* person with whom they could spend the rest of their lives.

But none of these admirably logical and sensible thoughts came anywhere near entering her head now as she simply stood and returned the intensity of Guy's silent visual contact with her.

Outside in the street, in the rest of the world, people went about their normal daily business, but the two of them were as far removed from that kind of mundanity as it was possible to be, transported to a world of their own where only the two of them existed.

Chrissie could feel her pulse jumping, her heart beating with frantic haste, her breathing growing far too fast and shallow, as she and Guy continued to search one another's face, the recognition between them both instant and compelling.

That he was good-looking and very physically male she had noted automatically when she opened the door, but her reaction to him now went deeper than that, much, much deeper. It encompassed not just his outward appearance, his physical attributes, but his deeper inner self, as well.

It was almost as though there was some psychic, soul-deep bond between them that both of them had instantly recognised and responded to. There could surely be no other reason for the sheer intensity of their shared sense of recognition and awareness, Chrissie reasoned as she mechanically stepped back into the cottage knowing that Guy would follow her in.

Guy couldn't believe what was happening to him. He knew there was a story within the family that along with the physical genes inherited from their wild Gypsy ancestor, there were those Cookes who also inherited some of his more spiritual and psychic gifts, but *he* had never had any occasion in the past to consider himself one of those so gifted, nor indeed to put very much credence in their existence.

He was far too much a modern twenty-first-century

man for that, and yet he was intensely aware of that startling moment of unexpected insight he had experienced when the cottage door opened and he had seen *her* standing there, had known the moment he looked at her that he was confronting his own fate. Somehow he already knew just how that wonderful waterfall of dark red hair would feel slipping through his hands, against his body…how *she* would feel, how she would taste, how she would smell and even how she would look…cry out in the moment of their shared physical coming together. He knew…he knew…

He could hear the blood pulsing in his ears and feel the rapid-fire volley of his heartbeat that sounded like a warning drum roll. He knew as he looked at her that she was *the* woman, the *one* woman, who would make his life—him—complete. He knew, too, that if he were to stretch out his hand to her now, she would put her own into it and silently follow him; allow him to lead her…*take* her, in every sense of the word, but she was no dependent, naïve clinging vine. On the contrary, he recognised that she was an extremely well-grounded and femininely powerful woman.

As he stepped into the hallway and closed the door behind him, he reached out instinctively to touch her face. Immediately Chrissie turned her head and pressed her mouth to the hard palm of his hand.

Guy heard himself groan as he drew her towards him with his other hand. Her body fitted perfectly within his, as he would fit perfectly within hers.

He didn't know which of them was trembling harder as he bent his head and replaced the hard warmth of his palm against her lips with the even harder warmth of his mouth. He only knew that the

tiny, agonized sound of delight she made beneath his
kiss was echoed a thousandfold deep within his own
body.

Chrissie could feel herself trembling violently as
she gave herself over not just to Guy's kiss, but to
the new role that fate had devised for her. She had
never imagined minutes ago when she opened the
door to him that she was opening the door to her
future. She had never been the kind of woman to rush
into any kind of physical intimacy—just the opposite—yet here she was, knowing that no matter how
far the intimacy went between the two of them, it
could be nowhere near as intense as the silent, emotional bonding they had already shared.

Never had she imagined that she could react like
this to a man's touch, to his kiss, that she could want
him so immediately and so overwhelmingly, that she
could feel the urgent almost violent desire within him
to tear aside the barriers of their clothing and know
her utterly and completely and to share that desire, to
know just how much he ached for the feel of her skin
against his, beneath his, and how much she shared and
returned that ache.

She could hear him whispering beneath their shared
hungry kisses how much he wanted her, how much
he had longed for her in his life—unintelligible, dis-
jointed words that ran together from a raw trickle of
sound into a sensual flood.

How long they stood there, kissing, touching…
wanting, Chrissie had no idea; she only knew that
when he finally released her, she was trembling so
much she could hardly stand up, that her mouth felt

swollen and bruised, that his mouth looked...
looked...

She swallowed as she looked at him and he reached
reassuringly for her hand, then held it tenderly in the
firm, warm grip of his own. '*Coup de foudre*, I believe
the French call it.'

'They would,' Chrissie replied shakily. She ached
to be back in his arms. She ached all over for him,
she admitted, inside and out, and it was nothing like
the aches and pains she had been suffering because
of her hard physical work cleaning up the cottage,
nothing at all.

God, but he wanted her, Guy recognised. He
wanted her so much that he didn't know how he was
managing to keep his hands off her. He had never
considered himself to be a highly sexed man, but right
now...

'I've never experienced anything like this before,'
Chrissie confessed.

'Good,' Guy told her tautly, adding rawly, 'I think
I'd want to kill any other man who might have—'

Chrissie stopped him, shaking her head, but she
knew what he meant. She felt equally savage and un-
characteristically jealous of any other woman who
might have had the same effect on him as she quite
obviously had had.

She took a deep breath and forced herself to try to
come back down to normality, but it was almost impossible. 'I want you so much,' she admitted shakily.
Then Guy was bridging the small gap between them
and taking her back in his arms.

For several long minutes, the only sound was that
of their increasingly passionate kisses and strained

breathing. Chrissie had no idea which of them it was
who lifted Guy's hand to her breast; she only knew
that the sensation of his holding her, touching her
there, made her whole body jerk in a frenzy of physical need, a sensation like a jolt of electricity running
straight from her breast to her womb, convulsing her
whole body with a deep-rooted, aching need.

'Please don't, please don't,' she whispered huskily,
even though she was the one who arched back against
him, guiding his hand whilst he rubbed the tip of his
thumb over and over her T-shirt-covered nipple until
she was pleading frantically with him to soothe her
aching flesh with the healing suckle of his mouth.

Chrissie had never pleaded with a man to make
love to her before or imagined she might want to, but
this whole situation was a world apart from anything
she had experienced before, completely foreign terri-
tory to her, a place where the old rules, the old guide-
lines, meant nothing and where the only things she
had to guide her were her own senses and needs and
his.

When Guy tugged up her T-shirt in response to her
frenzied pleas and fastened his mouth on the hard,
swollen tip of her breast, Chrissie almost felt she
might faint from the intensity of her pleasure.

She could hear his soft murmurs as he caressed her
and could feel the need in his body. She ached to
touch him, to explore him, to know him, and suddenly
the fierce suckling of his mouth against her breast
wasn't enough to satisfy the urgent clamour of her
physical response to him. Only one thing, one person,
could satisfy and silence that.

Her hands trembling, she lifted them to cup his face

and gently ease him away from her body. As he looked into her eyes, she dropped her hands and held one of them out to him and started to walk towards the stairs.

Her hand felt small and delicate, almost lost within the grip of his as he let her lead him, but as they started to mount the stairs, she felt him pull back slightly from her.

'You don't have to do this, you know,' she heard him telling her rustily.

Silently Chrissie searched his face before telling him with quiet dignity, 'Yes, I do, but if *you* would rather not...'

Her honest directness made Guy's heart ache for her. She was so trusting, so giving, so...so perfect.

'You shouldn't need to ask,' he told her huskily, adding with a rueful, self-derogatory laugh as he looked briefly down at his own body, 'The answer is, I'm afraid to say, rather too obvious.'

Chrissie couldn't help it. She followed his gaze, her eyes widening in betrayal of her female response to the evidence of his male desire for her. A tiny kick of pleasure pushed up her heart rate and the temptation to reach out and run her fingertips exploratively along the hard ridge of his arousal was one she had to fight hard to resist, but her body language had already given her away and Guy's visual reciprocal inspection of her was every bit as revealing of his own need.

For the first time in her life, Chrissie suddenly knew what it meant to feel sexually proud of her body, to know within the most inner core of herself that when she stood naked before Guy, it would be with pride and in the knowledge that her body, her femininity, her womanliness, would fill him with silent awe, with reverence, with arousal and need. As his nakedness would her.

She could feel his hand trembling slightly as she led the way to the small empty bedroom she was using.

Just for a second and only for a second as she opened the door and led him inside, she regretted the bareness of the scrubbed walls and floor, the plainness of the inflatable mattress with its simple white covering of bed linen she had brought from home. What, after all, did they need with the gaudy trappings of romance, with satin sheets and four-poster beds, rich brocades and thick carpets? They had all the richness, all the luxury, all the sensuality, they would need in one another.

Guy surveyed the plain bare room in silence. It smelled of fresh air and cleanliness and something far less easy to pigeon-hole—a scent, a perfume, an essence, which he recognised was hers.

'You're actually staying here?' he commented, frowning slightly as he did so. The house was in one of the poorer parts of town, and whilst Haslewich was, generally speaking, a safe enough place to live and safer than most, there had been several incidents lately of youths brawling in the streets in this part of town and it was only a couple of streets away trouble had erupted recently with youngsters apparently buying drugs outside a local nightclub.

'It seemed to be the most sensible thing to do,' Chrissie told him.

Was he perhaps put out by the starkness of the

room and its setting or did he perhaps think that she was being too forward and usurping his role? He wasn't to know, after all, how unique this whole situation was for her, how unique her desire for him and her responsiveness to him were, how unique he was.

'If you'd rather...' she began hesitantly, but Guy didn't let her finish.

He gathered her up in his arms as he told her softly, 'No. this is perfect...*you* are perfect. This is how love should be, not contrived or forced, achievable only with the right backcloth, the right props, the right setting, but simply instinctive and natural, wholesome and clean. We don't need any of the trappings of seduction, because this isn't seduction. And besides, no setting however beautiful could anywhere near match your beauty or the beauty of what we're going to share, to create.'

Chrissie felt her eyes start to fill with emotional tears. It was almost as though he could read her mind, as though he shared her thoughts, as though the two of them were so much in harmony that they were already almost a part of one another.

Unsteadily she lifted her hand to his face, touching her fingertips to his mouth, trembling as she explored the difference between the slightly rough flesh above his lip where he shaved with the sensual smoothness of his mouth.

'Chrissie.'

Slowly, one by one, he sucked her fingers into his mouth as he looked deep into her eyes.

As she looked equally intensely back at him, Chrissie had no awareness of the soft keening sound of pleasure she gave in response to the sensation caused by the sensually rhythmic movement of his mouth and tongue as they caressed her fingers.

Deep within her body, she could feel herself starting to ache and melt, to experience feelings and needs as old as humankind itself. Her body suddenly felt as though it were weighted down with heavy, inhibiting armour, her clothes a chafing restriction against which her skin and her senses rebelled.

In the past, sexual intimacy for Chrissie had always been a fairly passive activity with the man taking the lead. She had certainly never envisaged a situation where she might do as she was doing now and start to tug impatiently at her own irritatingly unyielding clothes in her yearning hunger to experience a man's hands on her body. But then, this was different...this was... Her small moans of frustration gave way to voluptuous sighs of pleasure as Guy started to help her remove her recalcitrant garments.

It shocked her a little at first to recognise when she finally stood naked before him that the unfamiliar scent of her body was the scent of her arousal, her desire for him, but if she found the realisation unexpected and slightly shocking, Guy, it seemed, viewed it in a totally different way and had no inhibitions about telling and showing her.

As he nuzzled the hollow between her breasts, he told her appreciatively, 'You smell so good. Just like a woman should.'

'I...there is a shower,' she began to suggest, but as though he guessed what she was thinking, Guy smiled slowly at her, then shook his head and told her firmly, 'No. Don't you know how erotic it is...how erotic you are...how much the scent of you makes me want to touch you, taste you, explore and know every inch of you?'

For the first time since that initial contact when they had looked into one another's eyes and known, Chrissie felt slightly flustered and uncertain.

'I don't want you all washed and antiseptic,' Guy added meaningfully. 'I want you the way you are now. A woman, warm and aroused, wanting me and scented by…tasting of that wanting…and I want you to want me in the same way,' he finished rawly.

'I do,' Chrissie whispered back, and she knew as she said it that it was true and that already she ached for the scent of him in her nostrils, the taste of him on her mouth.

Once again her eyes gave her away and Guy muttered hoarsely to her, 'You know what I mean, don't you?'

The only thing she needed to do was simply to nod her head and watch in trembling anticipation as he swiftly removed his own clothes. His body was taut and athletic, all clean lines and strong muscles. The sight of the soft, dark body hair that lay in silken whirls against his skin seized her body with a pang of female appreciation and made her curl her toes in sensual response to such masculinity.

Again in direct contradiction to her previous and admittedly rather prosaic and mundane sexual experience, she discovered that with Guy she actually wanted to look at his body, to explore it visually with an open-eyed female curiosity, not just to know its differentness but, she suspected with a small sense of shock, to inspect and judge its male ability to satisfy

the hunger that she knew she wasn't going to be able
to control for much longer.

She hadn't realised quite how long she had been
studying him or quite how hard she was frowning
until she heard Guy asking her with rueful light-
heartedness, 'Do I pass?'

Thoroughly mortified, Chrissie started to look
away, nodding her head as self-consciousness began
to overwhelm her, but Guy simply laughed and
hugged her reassuringly.

'It's all right,' he told her warmly. 'You have every
right to look and judge. There mustn't be any barriers
between us, Chrissie, or any inhibitions or murky
areas that can't be touched. That isn't what you and
I are about. Of course you want to look at me. Just
as I want to look at you. After all, doesn't half the
pleasure in enjoying a meal come from its visual presentation, and doesn't that presentation stimulate and
increase our appetite for it, just as looking at you is
stimulating my appetite for you?' he asked her softly.

And then, before she could make any response, he
bent his head to kiss her.

Gently at first, almost too gently, Chrissie decided,
she started to press herself closer to him whilst she
tried to prolong and deepen each kiss like a fish chas-
ing a lure, not realising that *she* was the one being
lured until Guy's arms snapped tightly round her and
then the tongue she had been trying yearningly to caress and coax with hers was suddenly no longer teasingly tempting her into his but instead thrusting pow-
erfully and sensually within her own, causing her
whole body to jerk against Guy's in a shudder of
pleasure she was completely unable to control.

Not, or so it seemed from Guy's approving reaction, that he wanted her to control it, or anything else, she recognised as his hands swept her body and cupped her buttocks, pulling her tightly against him whilst he murmured against her mouth how much he wanted her, how much he ached for her.

No more than she wanted and ached for him, Chrissie knew, but she wasn't aware of having whispered the words against his mouth until Guy picked her up in his arms and carried her across to the bed.

As he placed her on it, she could feel the warmth of his breath against the skin of her midriff. Shakily she closed her eyes as she felt herself starting to quiver and then tensed as she felt Guy's mouth brush lightly against her body, his tongue tracing round her navel.

Once and then again, a thousand tiny darts of sensual pleasure exploded inside her like the seeds of a puff-ball exploding in the summer sunshine, the sensation at one and the same time so delicate and yet so powerful that it shocked her into speechless wonder.

'Is it good?' she heard Guy questioning her thickly. 'Do you like that?'

Like it? The only reaction Chrissie could manage was a soft groan followed by a sharply indrawn breath as his mouth started to move downwards across her stomach towards her hip-bone in a series of caresses so light that they barely seemed to graze the surface of her skin and yet so sensually erotic that what lay beneath that skin was already reacting to them with a rhythmic urgency that couldn't be ignored.

Not even the sensation of his hand gently and protectively covering her sex could detract from the effect the delicate, tender exploration of his mouth was having on her body.

Which, she decided later, had to be the reason why she finally opened her eyes and saw Guy kneeling between her thighs, his whole concentration focused on the feminine heart of her as he slid his hands beneath her and gently tilted her body upwards so that he could have complete and total access to her intimacy. She felt no sense of inhibition or false modesty, no need to cover herself or push him away, but instead a strong awareness of the rightness, the perfection of his intimate, loving possession of her as his tongue probed the moist mystery of her body whilst she lay still and watchful, her breathing shallow but steady until he found what he was seeking and started to caress it with increasingly sensual strokes. Then her body trembled and jerked wildly in response to him, so wildly that she could feel the hard grip of his fingers biting possessively into her flesh as he continued to hold her beneath his mouth whilst she writhed and arched frantically beneath him, not sure if she wanted to pull away and bring her sweet torture to an end or arch up greedily against him and demand even more of the shocking pleasure he was giving her.

Her body, though, was perfectly sure of what *it* wanted, needed, craved, and the high female sound of arousal that sobbed from her throat made sure that Guy knew, as well.

'No. No more, please don't,' Chrissie panted deliriously as the hot quivers of pleasure darted through her body, convulsing her womb with tiny warning spasms of what lay ahead of her, making her shiver in a mixture of awe that she could feel such intense pleasure and a self-protective fear of the inevitable loss of self-control, of *self* that would come with it.

It was Guy who now controlled her body and her reactions and not her.

'Stop,' she begged him, adding unintentionally, 'I'm afraid...'

'Of what?' Guy asked her rawly. 'This?' He watched her face as she trembled against his touch.

'It's all so overpowering, so...so unfamiliar to me,' Chrissie admitted unwillingly. 'I don't...I haven't...'

'You've given yourself physically before,' Guy guessed for her, 'but not like this, not totally, completely, physically, emotionally and mentally, the way it is now between us. I feel just as afraid,' he told her simply, 'afraid of not matching up to your expectations, of disappointing you, of spoiling what we have been given.'

'You couldn't do that,' Chrissie told him softly, and as she said it she knew it was true and she knew something else, as well. 'I want you, Guy,' she told him emotionally, reaching out towards him, her body trembling as she met the burning look of physical desire in his eyes.

Unable to stop herself, she reached out and touched the tip of his erect manhood with her fingertips and then ran them slowly and a little hesitantly along the shaft.

Now it was his turn to tremble and groan, the sound emerging from deep within his chest as he closed his eyes and told her thickly, 'God, that feels so good, too good.' He suddenly tensed and groaned again, then bent his head and cupped her breast with his hand, drawing her nipple into his mouth and sucking fiercely on it, not just to give her pleasure, Chrissie recognised with a sharp kick of female power, but also because it was what he wanted. He needed to feel the soft warmth of her breast within his mouth, to draw on it and from it in just the same way that she now ached to feel him within her.

'Now, now, please, Guy, now,' she pleaded, whispering the impassioned words between the frantic kisses, her earlier fear of losing control completely forgotten, overwhelmed by a far more urgent and important need—the need to complete the cycle they had both set in motion, to be fulfilled, to be—

Chrissie gave a sharp, piercing cry of relief as she felt Guy's first deep thrust within her body.

'You feel wonderful,' she heard Guy telling her thickly. 'We fit together perfectly, perfectly.'

Chrissie couldn't make any verbal response but she knew there was no need, the way her body was already responding to the rhythmic movement of his told him everything he needed to know.

She had never imagined that physical intimacy could be like this; that two bodies could be so well matched, fit together so perfectly that they together made one perfect whole; so completely in harmony with one another that Chrissie actually felt as though she could physically feel the ripples of pleasure that ran through Guy's body with each movement he made within her own, and she sensed that he, too, could feel hers, that he knew exactly the second when she needed the more urgent movement of his body within hers, the heartbeat of time precisely even before she cried out to him that she ached for him, craved him, had to have him, deep, deep within the most secret part of her body.

And she could feel through the strong contractions of her own release the thick pulse of his.

'Oh, Guy,' Chrissie wept emotionally as he held her in his arms.

'I know. I know,' he soothed her tenderly, gently brushing the tears from her face as he bent his head to kiss her mouth lingeringly. He drew her deep into the protective warmth of his own body, stroking her skin as though he couldn't bear the thought of letting her go.

'You feel so good, so right,' he told her emotively. 'Oh God, you feel so good.'

'I still can't quite believe what's happened,' Chrissie confessed, suddenly a little shy. 'It's not...I don't...'

'Do you think I don't *know* that?' Guy interrupted her gruffly, taking hold of her hand and lifting it to his lips whilst he placed a kiss in her palm and then closed her fingers over it. 'And besides, what you and I have goes way, way beyond anything like any coy, false need to play games with one another. What we have...what we *can* have...' He broke off and shook his head. As she looked at him, Chrissie saw that his own eyes were filled with moisture.

'Oh, Guy,' she protested shakily. It was her turn now to comfort him, so she kissed his mouth with all the love she felt for him.

'We need to make time to talk to one another properly,' Guy told her unsteadily when she had released his mouth. 'No, not here,' he told her, reading her mind. 'If I stay here with you...' He groaned and closed his eyes. 'Have dinner with me tonight. My sister and her husband own a small restaurant. We could meet there. I daren't offer to pick you up,' he told her softly, 'because if I do…' He looked expressively at her still-naked body, warm and relaxed from his lovemaking, satiated…now…

But Guy was right. They *did* need to talk. There was so much she wanted to know about him, so much she wanted to discover.

'How ironic that I should meet you here of all places, in the house that belonged to Charlie Platt,' Guy murmured to her. When he saw Chrissie start to frown, he explained, 'We never got on.'

'You didn't like him,' Chrissie supplied, turning away slightly so that he couldn't see her face.

'No, I *didn't* like him,' Guy agreed grimly. 'In fact…' He stopped and shook his head. 'Let's not talk about Charlie Platt. He doesn't mean anything to either of us, thank God.'

Chrissie opened her mouth to tell him, correct him. 'Guy,' she began, but then got no further.

'I love the way you say my name,' he told her lovingly. 'It makes me want to kiss you like this….'

'You still haven't looked at the furniture,' Chrissie managed to remind him breathlessly, ten minutes later.

'I'll go through everything another time,' Guy responded, his expression suddenly changing, his eyes becoming dark and almost brooding as he asked her huskily, 'There *will* be another time, won't there, my Chrissie, and another and another and…?' Then he was kissing her again, and between those kisses Chrissie somehow found the breath to reassure him that their times together would stretch to eternity and beyond.

It took them over an hour to shower and dress and finally manage to say goodbye.

Chrissie had written down the address of his sister's restaurant, and after he had gone she simply sat and looked at it, already counting the minutes and the seconds until they could be together again.

The telephone rang whilst she was still engrossed in her day-dream, still floating on a cloud of pure golden bliss.

She smiled dreamily into the telephone as she picked up the receiver and responded to her mother's hello.

'You sound happy,' her mother commented.

'I am,' Chrissie told her simply and then proceeded to give her a very edited version of the events of the afternoon.

Chrissie was very close to her parents and kept no secrets from them, but she was just beginning to discover that some things were so precious, so sacred that they couldn't be shared with anyone other than the person they most closely concerned.

'I know it sounds incredible,' Chrissie told her mother, 'and I have to admit that if anyone had told me that Guy and I were going to fall in love at first sight, I probably wouldn't have believed them but—'

'Oh, Chrissie, are you sure...I don't think...' her mother interrupted her uncertainly. 'He sounds wonderful, darling, and of course I'm thrilled for you, but...'

'He's wonderful,' Chrissie assured her mother. 'He's more than wonderful,' she added softly, more to herself than to her parent. 'He knew Uncle Charles, by the way, although I got the impression that he didn't much care for him.'

'Did you tell him that Charles was your uncle?' her mother asked her anxiously.

'No. I didn't get the chance,' Chrissie told her. 'He's taking me out to dinner tonight, though, so I shall probably tell him then.'

There was a small pause before her mother queried doubtfully, 'Do you think that's wise, darling? I hate to pour cold water on things, but you said yourself that he didn't seem to have a very good opinion of your uncle and it might be wise not to say too much about your…your relationship with him, at least until the two of you get to know one another a little better.'

'You mean I should lie to Guy?' Chrissie questioned her mother, a little shocked.

'Well, no, of course not…at any rate not directly,' her mother responded. She paused. 'I should hate to think that your uncle's bad reputation might cast a shadow on your happiness, darling, and perhaps I shouldn't even suggest such a thing, but people do tend to make judgements. Of course, once your Guy has got to know you a little better, then…'

'Are you trying to say that Guy might reject me because of who…because of Uncle Charles?' Chrissie asked her mother slowly.

'I don't know, darling. I would hope not, but…well, your uncle…'

She didn't say any more; she didn't need to. Her uncle, as Chrissie well knew, had been a liar, a cheat and a thief.

'But I've upset you,' Chrissie heard her mother saying sadly, 'and that was the last thing I wanted to do....'

'No, no, it isn't that,' Chrissie tried to reassure her. 'It's just...well, I hate the thought of being deceitful...dishonest with anyone, but most especially with Guy.' But the idea that anything, anything at all, might cast the smallest shadow on her happiness filled her with such anguish, made her so fearful for the vulnerability of her newly born love that she instinctively wanted to protect it from anything and everything that might threaten or damage it.

'Did you ask your Guy to value the desk,' her mother prompted her whilst Chrissie blushed, remembering just why she hadn't even thought about mentioning the desk to him.

'No...no, I didn't,' she admitted. 'But perhaps under the circumstances it might be better to ask someone else to value it,' she suggested. 'I wouldn't want Guy or anyone else to think that I wanted him to value it in our favour because of...well, you understand what I mean,' she tried to explain.

'Yes, yes, of course,' her mother agreed. 'And you're quite right. It's the sentimental value of the desk that makes it so valuable to me and your father. We both agree we want to pay its full market value into the estate, even though by law I suspect that it's half my property anyway. Of course, it might be hard to prove as much. However, when I think of all those poor people your uncle defrauded...'

Chrissie didn't say anything. She already knew of her parents' decision to obtain via the solicitors acting for her deceased uncle a list of all her uncle's creditors so that these could be reimbursed—from her parents' own pocket in all probability. Chrissie doubted that even after the sale of the house and paying off the mortgages on it there would be enough to pay his debts.

'So anyway,' her mother teased gently as Chrissie started to bring their conversation to a close, 'when are we going to meet your Guy?'

'Not yet,' Chrissie told her firmly. 'Not until you get back from your trip—I'll be thinking about you tomorrow when you fly out.' She was glad that her mother couldn't see her flushed face as she acknowledged that whilst it was natural and automatic for her to discuss her feelings for Guy with her mother, they were still too new, he was still too new in her life, for her to want to share him publicly with anyone else.

'A table for two... What happens if I say we don't have one?' Frances Sorter teased her brother.

She had been a little uncertain at first just how things would work out between her husband and her brother when Guy had first offered to help finance their restaurant business. Both of them were in their own quiet way rather dominant, the kind of males who were used to being in control and taking command. But as she acknowledged now, she needn't have worried.

The two men got along just fine and there was no doubt that Guy contributed some valuable input into the business and not just in terms of money or even the business he brought in. It had been Guy who had encouraged them to expand and extend the dining room when they had been a little wary of taking on the extra financial commitment, and Guy, too, who had backed his faith in them with the money to do so. And he had been right. The plain, old-fashioned but superbly cooked country food that her husband specialised in had very quickly met with local approval and they were already gaining an equally good reputation farther afield, as well.

Roy, her husband, insisted on using only top-quality ingredients, organically grown vegetables and livestock reared by traditional methods rather than factory farmed. His beefsteak pie had male customers salivating in anticipation and their wives complaining that they were tired of having their home cooking compared to its detriment with Roy's.

'Paul even told me that Roy's pastry was better than his mother's,' one wife had confided ruefully to Frances.

Both their sons were now at catering college and hopefully would eventually come into the business with them, while Miranda, their daughter, had set up her own ancillary sideline, catering for private dinner parties and the like and keeping to the family tradition of serving wholesome country food.

'Is it a business dinner?' Frances asked, pausing delicately.

Guy looked at her. 'No,' he told her quietly.

'No...? It's a woman,' Frances guessed.

'She's a woman,' Guy agreed, only just resisting the temptation to tell his sister she was *THE* woman. However, he knew her too well and he knew also that once he had said that, every member of the Cooke clan would know by this time tomorrow what he had told her and he wasn't ready for that, not quite yet. He wanted her to himself far too much right now to want to share her with anyone else, much less his inquisitive, gregarious and sociable family.

'Oh, I almost forgot to tell you,' Frances exclaimed. 'There's been another break-in—at The Limes this time. Apparently the police suspect that a professional gang's at work.'

Guy knew that his sister's husband's cousin was a police inspector based in Chester and so he listened frowningly as she provided him with details.

'The police suspect that the gang moves into an area and picks it clean before moving on. They're not going for the really valuable stuff—that's too heavily protected and alarmed—but apparently they do seem to know what they're looking for. Chester, of course, with all its antiques shops and its visitors is an ideal place for them to get rid of what they've stolen by offloading it to dealers before the police can circulate a description of what's gone.'

'Mmm. It's every dealer's nightmare,' Guy agreed, 'to find out that what you've bought in good faith turns out to be stolen property.'

'How are things going for the Antiques Fair?' Frances asked him, changing the subject.

'Fine,' Guy responded, adding with a grin, 'Almost too well at the moment, in fact. So far, my major problem is finding enough space for everyone who wants to participate and I've actually had to turn down quite a few.'

'A bit different from the first one you organised three years ago,' his sister reminded him. 'Then, you were virtually having to plead with people to come.'

'Don't remind me,' Guy told her wryly.

'You still made a success of it, though,' she pointed

out. 'And a good profit, plus what was donated to local charities. Will you be doing that again this year?'

'Oh yes, I don't think that either Jenny or Ruth would let me get away with not doing.'

Frances laughed. 'Ruth Crighton's homes for single mothers is a very worthwhile cause,' she pointed out to her brother, 'and because it's small and local I think that people do feel more inclined to want to help. Ruth was telling me the last time she and Grant were here that they're actually starting to train their own counsellors and planning to provide an after-care service for their mothers and babies.'

'Tell me about it,' Guy groaned. 'It's begun to take over so much of Jenny's time that I've got a feeling it won't be long before she decides to give up her share of the business.'

Frances gave him a sharp look. Guy and Jenny Crighton had been in business together for many years now, although she knew that for Jenny the antiques shop they both ran had never been more than a part-time sideline. She had occasionally wondered over the years about the exact nature of the relationship between her brother and Jenny, for although it was obvious that Jenny was devoted to her husband, Jon Crighton, the senior partner in the family's local legal practice, it was also obvious, to Frances at least, that Guy was extremely fond of and protective towards his business partner. Now though, totally unexpectedly it seemed, there was a new woman in Guy's life.

Frances was no fool. She was well aware that her brother had not exactly lived the life of a monk and that in his twenties in particular he had dated a string of stunningly attractive young women. But he was close to forty now and so far as she knew, there had been no one special in his life for quite some time. So who was this new woman and where had Guy met her? she wondered curiously. She would have to make some enquiries via the family grapevine, she decided vigorously, whilst giving her brother a dulcetly innocent smile.

CHAPTER FOUR

CHRISSIE had just stepped out of the bath when she heard someone knock on the door. Pulling on her towelling robe, she hurried downstairs and then paused warily before checking the safety catch and opening the door, her small frown of uncertainty dissolving in the heat of her delighted smile as she saw Guy standing on the doorstep, his arms full of flowers.

'You said we should meet at the restaurant,' she reminded him huskily after she had let him in and laughingly admonished him for the extravagance of the enormous armful of flowers he had given her.

'I know,' he agreed tenderly, giving her a look that made her toes curl and her body go hot.

'You said that if we didn't, that you…that we…' she began as she took the flowers into the kitchen where they totally filled the small sink.

'I know *exactly* what I said and why,' Guy asserted. As Chrissie turned round, he caught her in his arms and added gruffly, 'And I was right, too. God, I've missed you.'

'You can't have,' Chrissie protested shakily. 'It's only been a few hours and—'

'A few hours, a few minutes, it doesn't matter how long it is…any amount of time spent away from you is too long,' Guy interrupted her passionately.

It must be because she hadn't had anything to eat

since this morning that she felt so light-headed and dizzy, Chrissie told herself. Either that or…

'We'll be late for dinner,' she warned Guy as he started to kiss her, unfastening her robe so that he could slide his hands inside it and slowly caress her naked and still-damp body.

'Do you care?' he asked her throatily.

Chrissie shook her head.

This time, because she knew what to expect, she somehow assumed that her response would be less intense, the emotion between them not quite as magical, but she quickly discovered she was wrong. If anything, their response to one another, their need for one another, was even more total and overwhelming than it had been before, their bodies moving in perfect harmony with one another.

'I've never known anything like this,' Guy whispered rawly to her as he held her in the aftermath of their loving.

'Neither have I,' Chrissie agreed. 'It…it frightens me a little bit,' she told him quietly. 'It's almost…too perfect.…'

'*Too* perfect!' Guy laughed. 'How *can* it be?' he teased her.

Chrissie laughed as well, her laughter turning to a wide-eyed look of shaken passion as Guy started to make love to her again, bending his head to gently kiss and then caress the naked tip of her breast, slowly and delicately drawing the sensitive, responsive flesh into his mouth whilst Chrissie gasped in helpless pleasure, reaching out for him, clinging to him as she felt herself start to be caught up in the powerful undertow of the desire he was arousing within her.

'I'm never going to want to let you go now, you know that, don't you?' Guy told her tenderly after they had made love.

'I don't think I'm ever going to want you to let go,' Chrissie admitted honestly, closing her eyes, caught halfway between tears and laughter as her emotions overwhelmed her. 'I still can't quite believe that all this is happening,' she added. 'I only came to Haslewich to sort out my...things here.'

'You came because fate had already decreed that we should meet,' Guy corrected her softly.

'I...I wouldn't even *be* here if I wasn't representing...' Her voice tailed off. Despite what her mother had said to her, she knew she had to tell him the truth and explain exactly who she was.

But Guy had other things on his mind and Chrissie abandoned any attempt to talk to him as he started to kiss her—again!

'You're late and you're lucky we kept you a table,' his sister told Guy severely over two hours later when they finally made it to the restaurant.

Standing at his side, Chrissie was blushingly conscious of just how she must look and of just how many of the subtle and not-so-subtle signs of *how* they had spent the past few hours must be clearly evident.

No amount of make-up could possibly cover the tell-tale glow warming her skin or the softness of her eyes, the bee-stung, kiss-swollen shape of her mouth, the sensual languor that still possessed her body. And she was conscious, too, of the discreet but very thorough inspection Guy's sister was giving her.

Like him, she, too, was dark-haired with arresting

good looks. He had told Chrissie earlier when she had been unable to stop herself commenting with female appreciation on the powerful shape of his body and the dark golden warmth of his skin that he owed his physical appearance to the genes he had inherited from his Gypsy ancestor.

'Theirs was a relationship that caused quite a scandal at the time,' he had explained wryly and told her the story of how he came to have Gypsy blood in his veins and how, even now, as a family they were not always totally accepted by everyone locally.

'People in small towns have long memories and there was a time centuries ago when the description ''gypsy'' was synonymous with the word ''thief'', at least in some people's eyes. I want you to know exactly what you're getting,' he had added, watching her. 'Good *and* bad, because, make no mistake, my love, I mean to be a permanent part of your life, a *very* permanent part of your life.'

Chrissie had been too overwhelmed with emotion to make any coherent response or to tell him about her own family.

'He's definitely in love with her,' Frances exclaimed positively to her husband once she had shown them to their table and returned to the kitchen. 'You can tell just by the way he looks at her.'

'Of course you can,' her husband scoffed. 'Fran, Guy is damn near forty and to the best of my knowledge he's had any number of women running after him, yes and he's let a good few of them catch him as well and...'

'This is different,' his wife interrupted him firmly, tutting in disgust at his male lack of perception. She glanced at her watch and wondered if there was time to make a few phone calls. The rest of the family were going to be interested in what she had to tell them.

'You're going to have to stop looking at me like that or we'll have to leave,' Guy warned her.

'Looking at you like what?' Chrissie asked.

But of course she knew. It made her feel giddy, light-headed, light-years away from her real self, to know that she could barely take her gaze away from his mouth, his body...his... Her *real* self?

'Stop it,' she begged him huskily when he returned her look with an open sensuality that made her whole body go hot. 'We've got to be sensible,' she told him. 'We—'

'Sensible?' he queried ruefully. 'That's the last thing I feel like being, but I suppose you have a point. I don't even know how long you're going to be here or—'

'I don't know myself yet,' Chrissie told him. 'I've got an appointment with Jon Crighton tomorrow.'

'Jenny's husband,' he interjected, adding, 'Jenny Crighton is my partner in the antiques shop.'

Chrissie frowned. Something about the way he said the other woman's name and the way he looked struck a disconcerting warning note.

'Presumably you're acting for the Platt family. It's hardly surprising that they didn't want to deal with things personally.'

'They can hardly be blamed for what...for what Charles did,' Chrissie protested defensively.

'No, but this is a small town and people have long memories and narrow minds, as my family has good cause to know. Charlie treated a lot of people very badly and rightly or wrongly anyone turning up here now and claiming to be related to him is bound to be treated with suspicion.'

'Is that what you would do?' Chrissie asked him a little stiffly.

Guy smiled at her as he reached across the table to take hold of her hand and shrugged. 'Does it matter? If I'm honest, I don't suppose I would be inclined to look charitably on another member of the Platt family, but right now neither Charlie Platt nor anyone else is of the remotest interest to me. In fact, right now, there is only one person on my mind....' He smiled into her eyes tenderly. 'Right now, the only person I want to think about or talk about is you....'

'There isn't anything to tell,' Chrissie fibbed uncomfortably. How *could* she tell him who she was after what he had just said? 'I'm here to represent the Platt family and I've got to see his solicitors and get the house put up for sale.'

'Well, Jon Crighton will help you do all that. His family have been the town's solicitors for heaven knows how many years now. In fact, the original Crighton connection with the law goes back even beyond that, to Chester, where Jon's ancestor actually came from.

'There are still Crightons practising as barristers and solicitors in Chester. And Jon and Jenny's elder son, Max, is presently a practising barrister in London. They're quite an extended clan, not quite so extensive as the Cookes, of course, but then, we have the advantage of our extremely prolific Gypsy genes to thank or blame for our colonisation of the town.'

Prolific! How prolific? Chrissie wondered uneasily, suddenly acutely conscious of something she had neglected to discuss with Guy in the fierce immediacy of their need for one another. Something she was now shamefully aware she *should* have mentioned, checked...insisted upon, out of practical considerations and health-conscious maturity, if nothing else. But she had been too overwhelmed, too hungry for the feel of Guy inside her to spare a thought for something so practical, and Guy, she suspected, must have felt exactly the same.

'Is something wrong?' she heard him asking her quietly.

Quickly she shook her head. The contraceptive pills she had been prescribed to regulate her monthly cycle would normally have protected her, but she was guiltily aware that her most recent prescription was still unfilled in her purse and she had taken her last pill a few days ago. First thing in the morning, she would make sure she went to the chemist's, she promised herself.

'Er...no...nothing,' she assured him, too distracted by the realisation that his sister was walking towards them to tell him what was bothering her.

'Is everything all right?' Frances asked Guy wryly, as she surveyed their barely touched, and now cold, food.

'Fine, but neither of us had much of an appetite,' Guy replied.

'Not for food,' Chrissie thought she heard the other woman murmur wryly as she gestured to a waitress to collect their plates.

'What time are you due to see Jon tomorrow?' Guy

asked as soon as his sister had gone. 'Only I'm due to visit Lord Astlegh's estate manager in the morning to check over things for the Antiques Fair I'm organising there and I wondered if you'd like to come with me. It's quite an interesting house with some spectacular gardens.'

'I'd love to,' Chrissie told him warmly. 'My appointment isn't actually until three…'

'Wonderful, we can have lunch together, somewhere a little more private,' he added ruefully.

His sister had sharper eyes than he had given her credit for, he acknowledged inwardly, and she had certainly guessed exactly how he felt about Chrissie. He suspected she would lose no time in passing her discovery on to the rest of their family.

'If you don't want anything else we could leave and have coffee somewhere a little quieter…'

Chrissie looked at him knowing that everything she was feeling was in her eyes. 'Yes… I'd like that,' she told him a little breathlessly.

She wasn't totally surprised when she discovered that he was taking her to his home, but her heart was thumping heavily when he guided her up the narrow pathway to the immaculately painted front door of the handsome, brick-built, three-storey terraced house with its Georgian façade.

They entered a narrow but high-ceilinged hallway off which Guy opened a door, flicking on the lights to illuminate an elegantly furnished sitting room carpeted in a neutral sisal matting that showed off perfectly the room's antiques and at the same time blended with the two large, squashy, creamy damask-

covered sofas that faced one another across the fire-
place.

'Make yourself at home,' Guy invited her. ' I'll go
and make some coffee.'

'I'll come with you,' Chrissie told him huskily, giving him a faintly tremulous smile as he extended his
hand towards her and drew her down the hallway.

It was so unlike her to be like this, to be so up front
and femininely demanding in her intense desire for
him. Words, feelings and desires she simply could not
contain seemed to have swept aside her normal cau-
tion and replaced it with emotions and needs so boldly
brilliant that they filled her whole consciousness,
blinding in that brilliance, in the same way that Guy's
presence seemed to fill the unexpectedly large and
well-planned kitchen he was now moving capably
about, opening cupboards, removing mugs, filling a
kettle.

Whilst he stood with his back to her, reaching up
into the cupboard above him for a jar of coffee,
Chrissie studied him openly, greedily absorbing the
satisfying sight of his body. His shoulders were broad,
tapering to a narrow waist, his legs long and lean,
topped with neat buttocks. And as she had good cause
to know, the flesh beneath his shirt would feel warm
and smooth, sheer heaven both to touch and kiss. She
was tempted to go over to him, wrap her arms round
him, tease his shirt out from his belt and...

'What is it, what's wrong?' Guy asked her with
concern, turning round just as the small yearning
sound she had been trying to suppress escaped her
lips.

'No, nothing,' she managed to tell him, but Guy

continued to frown slightly at her as he spooned the coffee into their mugs.

'Coffee's almost ready,' he announced unnecessarily as the kettle boiled. But Chrissie's mind was made up. After spending these past few pulse-rate-inflating minutes standing in his kitchen, watching him, absorbing his every movement, wanting him, she knew exactly what she ached for and needed, and it certainly *wasn't* a cup of coffee.

'No...' Chrissie shook her head, caught off guard both by the trembling of her body and the surge of desire that possessed her. 'I...I don't want anything to drink,' she murmured, then admitted honestly, 'I...I just want you.'

'Oh God, what *have* I done to deserve you?' Guy groaned as he took her in his arms and showed her just how thoroughly her feelings, her needs, were returned. 'You don't *know* how much I ache for you right now,' he breathed into her mouth.

'Show me,' Chrissie invited him, shamelessly winding her arms round his neck and pressing her body close to his.

Somewhere on the edge of her consciousness was a vague memory of something she ought to tell him, but so many more pressing needs were demanding her attention, and right now all she could think of was just how good that unmistakable hardness she could feel in his body would be once it was inside hers.

She had never felt so completely overwhelmed by her own physical needs before or by the urge to express and share them. Swiftly she dismissed the unwanted jarring voice that dared to try to spoil the perfection of her new-found love.

The bedroom he took her to upstairs was furnished with the same sturdily constructed antique country furniture she had admired in the sitting room, the centrepiece a fine four-poster oak bed.

'I did at one time think of making a career in interior design,' Guy confessed when Chrissie commented on how much she liked the clever combination of heavy, natural, masculine-looking fabrics he had used. 'We're sometimes called in as consultants by clients.'

'You chose the décor for the restaurant, didn't you?' Chrissie guessed, recalling that despite her preoccupation with Guy she had still been aware of the comfortable and easy ambience of the restaurant.

'Yes,' Guy agreed. 'Frances and Roy are planning to extend and add on a conservatory area for summer dining and private parties, and with that in mind I felt that the Mediterranean colours we used in the main eating area would blend best with that kind of exterior and the outside eating area Frances and Roy hope will go with it.

'I spent a couple of years living and working in Italy and I have to confess that they have the art of alfresco dining to perfection.'

'Italy…mmm…I spent several months there myself during my gap year. I loved Florence.'

Her gap year. Guy grimaced inwardly. The idea of a gap year either before or after university had been an unheard-of luxury when he had been that age. He had gone to Italy, driven by a restless urge to experience a different environment from the somewhat enclosed world he had grown up in, but he had had to work his way there—hard, dirty, manual work in the

main. He had worked in Italy, too, harvesting pota-
toes, working in bars and kitchens, doing anything
and everything he could to keep himself solvent.

Without her having to say, he already knew that
Chrissie came from a very different background from
his own; that she had grown up in a typical, com-
fortably affluent upper-middle-class household, where
her father had no doubt been in one of the professions
and her mother, if she had worked at all, had done
voluntary work for a pet charity. Chrissie herself had
probably gone to a private school.

He had sensed her reluctance to discuss her background and wondered if it was because she had
guessed how very different it was from his own. Class
differences in this modern age were supposed to be a
thing of the past, dead and gone, but of course they
were not.

His own parents, whilst thrifty and hard-working,
had had a lifestyle a world away from that enjoyed
by the upper middle classes.

His father had joined the navy after leaving
school—there was a tradition in the Cooke family of
its young men joining the armed services—and then
after he had met and married Guy's mother, he had
taken over the tenure of one of the town's public
houses—another family tradition.

It had been the restlessness inherited from his
Gypsy forebear that had spawned Guy's youthful
travel bug. The years spent travelling and working on
the continent had broadened his horizons, but there
was a part of him that was aware that despite his financial success, or maybe even because of it, there

was still a certain section of the town's population who treated him slightly warily.

'Tell me more about this antiques fair you're organising,' Chrissie commanded him sleepily as she snuggled deeper into his arms, her body relaxed and sated from their lovemaking.

'There isn't much to tell,' Guy protested, only half-truthfully.

As Jenny had remarked only the previous week, it had been an achievement in itself for him to have persuaded Lord Astlegh to agree to their using Fitzburgh Place as the venue for the fair, and of course it was that venue that attracted the very high quality of participators in the event.

Guy had been meticulous, too, in ensuring that only high-quality food outlets and caterers would be allowed to participate. The orchestra from a local music school had been engaged to play, along with a string quartet; traditional jugglers and other street acts in period costume would add a touch of liveliness and vibrant colour to the scene.

There had been a good deal of press interest both locally and nationally in the three-day event, which was to commence with a champagne reception hosted by the Lord Lieutenant of the county and held in the house itself.

'Organising the security for it must have been a real nightmare,' Chrissie commented as she snuggled even deeper into his arms and remembered the problems her mother had had in getting adequate insurance and security cover for one of her charity events.

'It certainly was,' Guy agreed dryly.

He had lost count of the number of meetings he
had had with the patient police inspector whose responsibility the event had become, and then there had
been the additional headache of hiring security staff
and even acquiring portable alarms.

'We can't provide for every eventuality,' he told
Chrissie, 'and ultimately it's the responsibility of
every participator to check the terms of their own insurance coverage and organise their own security if
they feel it's necessary. One of our biggest headaches,
in fact, has been getting the permission of insurers to
hold the event.'

'I suppose Lord Astlegh must own a considerable
amount of valuable antiques himself,' Chrissie commented.

'A very considerable amount,' Guy agreed. 'As
well as an exceptionally fine art collection and a good
deal of very rare porcelain.'

Chrissie, who had often helped her mother organise
her charity events, smiled sympathetically as she
leaned over to kiss him and then promptly forgot
about the Antiques Fair and everything else as he
kissed her back and proved to her own astonishment
that she wasn't quite as sleepy as she had thought after
all.

'Mmm...' Chrissie moved languorously against the
teasingly explorative hand stroking her body.

'Wake up, sleepyhead,' Guy instructed her. 'It's
gone nine o'clock in the morning.'

'What...?' Chrissie opened her eyes in disbelief. 'It
can't be,' she protested.

'See for yourself,' Guy told her with a smile, showing her his watch. 'Nine o'clock,' he repeated, 'and you've been snoring your head off.'

'Snoring?' Chrissie repeated indignantly as she sat up in bed, her indignation giving way to laughter as she realised that Guy was teasing her.

Threateningly she reached for her pillow but before she could aim it at him, Guy started to wrestle it from her. Only somehow or other it was her naked body his hands were touching and her own laughter died as she recognised the look in Guy's eyes and felt herself responding to it.

In the end, it was gone eleven o'clock before they finally set off for Fitzburgh Place, calling *en route* at Charlie's house so that Chrissie could change her clothes.

'Lord Astlegh is very good about allowing both the house and the grounds to be used for a variety of local functions,' Guy told Chrissie as she made him stop his car so she could take a longer look at the spectacular vista revealed by a sharp turn in the drive leading to the house.

'Aarlston-Becker held a particularly spectacular masquerade ball here not so long ago,' Guy added, smiling at her awed excitement.

They both surveyed the man-made canal that bisected the grounds to the front of the house and the ornamental lake complete with island and 'Greek' temple that lay beyond it.

'The original design for the grounds dates from the time of Charles II,' Guy explained, 'with certain modifications incorporated during the reign of William and Mary, hence the Dutch influence. Fortunately, when the fashion for Capability Brown's "natural vistas" was at its height, the then-incumbent of the house was more dedicated to the gaming tables than redesigning his gardens and so they remained untouched.'

'They're beautiful,' Chrissie acknowledged, then asked, 'Where exactly will the fair be held?'

'To the rear of the house, in the mews area round the original stable yard, which is separated from the house and which Lord Astlegh has had converted into a series of workshops that are let to local craftspeople at very low rents. He also provides them with access to business advice, which ranges from help in preparing their books and accounts to guidance on the best market products.'

'He sounds very philanthropic,' Chrissie commented.

'Well, yes, he is,' Guy agreed. 'But it's a move that several big landowners are following, adopting a trend originally started by the likes of the Duke and Duchess of Devonshire.'

They were back in the car now, but instead of heading towards the main house, Guy took a narrow drive that angled out to the rear of the property and steered through a pair of stout wooden doors set in a high brick wall and into the cobbled stable yard that lay behind it. As Guy brought the car to a halt, Chrissie caught her breath.

What she assumed had originally been stables had been converted into small, double-storey units, each with its own window and smartly painted dark green door flanked by Versailles planters filled with an artistic profusion of summer bedding plants.

Several other cars were already parked in the large

enclosed area, and as she studied her surroundings
Chrissie could see how well it would adapt to a traditional market-place environment, right down to the
smartly painted pump she noticed in the middle of the
yard.

'The barn at the end there will be cleared out to
house some of the exhibitors,' Guy was telling her as
he indicated the large building forming one side of
the rectangular area, 'while various empty units are
going to be converted to shops selling a variety of
traditional items. Stalls will be erected in the yard
itself and the original tack rooms and the space above
them will house a traditional market-place restaurant
and bar.'

'It's going to be wonderful,' Chrissie enthused,
genuinely impressed. 'The organisation must be causing you quite a few headaches, though,' she added.

'Just a few,' Guy agreed ruefully before bending
his head to whisper to her, 'but I think I've discovered
the perfect cure for them.'

Chrissie laughed.

'A headache is supposed to put you off sex,' she
reproved him. 'Not—'

'What you and I have is a long, long way from
mere sex,' Guy interrupted her seriously. 'A long,
long way.'

The look he gave her made Chrissie feel weak at
the knees.

Whilst Guy had his meeting with the estate manager,
Chrissie elected to go for a walk in the grounds. The
Greek temple on its small island in the middle of the
lake would make a very romantic venue for a wed-

ding, she decided dreamily as she sat cross-legged on a grassy knoll overlooking the lake. So much had happened in such a very short space of time that she was still half-inclined to feel she ought to pinch herself just to make sure that she was fully awake. It was now totally impossible for her to contemplate a life for herself that did not include Guy—her relationship with him, and the love they shared, as the focal point of that life.

'This is Chrissie,' he had said, introducing her to his sister last night, and then he had looked at her in a way that showed more clearly than any verbal explanation ever could just how he really felt about her.

'I think your sister guessed about us,' Chrissie had told him later when they were in bed.

'Mmm...I suppose I did rather give the game away,' Guy had admitted as he nibbled delicately on her ear. 'She'll probably have told the whole Cooke clan by now. I hope,' he added teasingly, 'you don't have any skeletons tucked away in your closet because if you do, knowing the female side of my family, they won't take very long to dig them out.'

'None at all,' Chrissie had assured him lovingly, but of course, it hadn't quite been the truth, had it? She still hadn't told him about Uncle Charles, and she must do. She would do. Tonight, she promised herself as she glanced at her watch and realised that Guy's meeting would be over.

She got to her feet and started to walk back towards the stable yard. When she got there, another car had been parked next to Guy's, and as she crossed the yard she saw that Guy was talking with an elegantly dressed woman who looked slightly older than Guy himself.

Both of them were deeply engrossed in their conversation, and from the proximity of their bodies and the affectionate, almost intimate way Guy had his hand on her shoulder and the way she was responding by, if not actively nestling up against him, then certainly standing extremely close to him, Chrissie guessed that their relationship was a long-standing one.

Long-standing and... She bit her lip as she recognised that the feeling paralysing her, making her stay where she was a good ten feet away, unwilling to intrude on their closeness, was one of acute and very painful jealousy.

And then Guy turned his head and saw her.

Was it her imagination or had she, for the barest fleeting breath of time, seen a look in his eyes that suggested that her arrival, her presence, wasn't entirely welcome? If so, it was gone now and there was certainly nothing in the way he was smiling at her to suggest that he wasn't pleased to see her—far from it.

'Chrissie,' he exclaimed, 'come and meet Jenny.'

Jenny! So this was his partner.... Jenny Crighton, Jon Crighton's wife. A little hesitantly, Chrissie went forward.

The other woman wasn't beautiful in the obvious physical sense and she certainly wasn't young, but despite that, she had a warmth, a sweetness...a certain something about her that Chrissie could see would appeal very much to a certain type of red-blooded male. And although there was nothing in Jenny's manner to suggest it when she smiled warmly at Chrissie and shook her hand, Chrissie also somehow knew that Jenny's feelings for Guy were far deeper and more complex than those of one business partner for another.

Was the atmosphere she could sense between the two of them a legacy from some past relationship or the result of something that existed in the present? If so, how might it affect her own relationship with Guy? She wasn't a jealous person by nature but then she had never felt about another man the way she did about Guy, she recognised.

'Jenny and I were just discussing some of the arrangements for the fair,' Guy explained to Chrissie, adding to Jenny, 'Chrissie is dealing with Charlie Platt's estate. We met when I went round to check over the contents.'

As Jenny extended her hand towards her, Chrissie took it somewhat reluctantly. It wasn't like her to feel awkward or uncomfortable with a member of her own sex, but for some reason she discovered that she couldn't quite meet Jenny Crighton's eyes.

Because she was afraid of what Jenny might see in her own eyes or because she was afraid of what Jenny's might reveal to her?

'Will Louise and Katie be able to help out at the fair this year?' Guy asked Jenny, then turned to Chrissie to enlighten her. 'Katie and Louise are Jon and Jenny's twin daughters.'

'No, I'm afraid not. They're both studying hard for their exams,' Jenny informed him. 'So they won't have much spare time on their hands.'

'Louise is still determined that she and Katie are going to become Eurolawyers, I take it?' Guy smiled.

'Louise is, but I rather think that Katie has her own ideas about her future,' Jenny returned wryly. 'Jon and I had hoped to spend a few days visiting them this month, but the break-in has affected Ben quite badly and we're a bit reluctant to leave him. Ben is my husband's father,' Jenny explained for Chrissie's benefit. 'Queensmead, his home, was broken into recently and although Ben himself wasn't aware of what was going on—fortunately he was asleep in bed at the time and the burglars didn't disturb him—it has left him feeling very vulnerable.'

'Your father-in-law must have been terribly shocked,' Chrissie sympathised.

Despite her disturbing suspicions about the depth of intimacy that existed between Guy and Jenny, she had to acknowledge that there was a friendliness and warmth about Jenny, which in other circumstances would have had her wanting to get to know the older woman better. As it was...

Turning away, she frowned as Guy started to describe his meeting with the estate manager to Jenny, aware that, although she wasn't being deliberately excluded from their conversation, it involved a part of Guy's life about which she had very little knowledge and, in fact, revealed rather painfully to her just how wide the gulf was between her knowledge of him and Jenny's.

She *had* known him less than twenty-four hours, she reminded herself sternly. He and Jenny had quite obviously known one another for years, but she still was sharply conscious of the fact that Guy had made no move to reach out and draw her closer or even to touch her physically in any way, whilst Jenny was standing close enough to him for their bodies to be touching.

'It's been very nice meeting you,' Jenny told her with a smile, having glanced at her watch and exclaimed that she had things to do.

'We ought to be getting on, too,' Guy observed, adding, 'Chrissie has an appointment with Jon this afternoon to sort out the legal ramifications of Charlie Platt's estate.'

'Oh yes,' Jenny said, smiling at Chrissie. Jon had mentioned to her over breakfast that he had an appointment with the late Charlie Platt's niece concerning his affairs.

Jenny shook hands with her, but she and Guy hugged and kissed one another with obvious closeness and affection, Chrissie noticed before the older woman turned and hurried away, leaving them heading for Guy's car at a more leisurely pace.

'You and Jenny have obviously known one another a long time,' Chrissie remarked as Guy drove back to town, unable to resist bringing up the subject even though she felt a stab of jealousy.

'Yes, we have,' Guy agreed, the warmth in his voice and the way he was smiling fanning the flames of Chrissie's apprehensions into an unwanted positive belief that Jenny held a very special place in his life— and in his heart?

'How long have she and Jon been married?' she asked, unwilling to demand to know outright just what Jenny meant to him and yet increasingly anxious to dispel her growing fears.

'I'm not quite sure. Well over twenty-five years,' Guy informed her. 'Max, their eldest child, must be in his late twenties, I should think.'

Over twenty-five years. Chrissie started to relax slightly. Well, at least that meant that there could have been no youthful relationship between Guy and Jenny, the embers continuing to smoulder throughout Jenny's marriage. But she still couldn't entirely relax.

'And they've always been happy together, have they?' she probed.

Guy frowned as he turned his head towards Chrissie. What on earth had made her ask that particular question and how the hell should he answer it?

The truth was that Jon and Jenny's marriage *had* gone through a bad patch at one time and he... His frown deepened.

The relationship between him and Jenny had never been anything other than that of business partners and good friends, but... But there had been a time when he had wanted it to be more, he acknowledged inwardly. There had, in fact, been a time when he had been ready and willing—more than willing, if he was being honest—to encourage Jenny to leave Jon... when he had actively wanted her to do so. Fortunately and wisely, Jenny had never allowed either of them to cross the fine line that divided the safety of friendship from the danger of...something else.

There was no logical reason why he couldn't tell Chrissie any of this. But how would she react to the knowledge that he had once come very close to wanting Jenny to break her marriage vows, to convincing himself that the emptiness he had been beginning to sense in his life at that time might be filled by her;

that her vulnerability and need had aroused within him a protective and very masculine desire to shelter and take care of her and to convince both himself and her that those emotions could be transmuted into something they could both call love.

Surely it was sufficient for *him* to know that he had been wrong and that thankfully Jenny had known that and prevented them both from making what he now knew would have been a bad mistake.

He would eventually, of course, tell Chrissie about Jenny and about his own awareness of how emotionally vulnerable he had been at that time. And he could tell her then, too, how glad he was at the same time that she was the only woman he had ever and could ever want to make a formal lifelong commitment to. That now that there *was* love, that now that he *did* love, he could recognise the vast gulf, the huge difference, that existed between it and what he had believed he felt for Jenny.

Yes, he would tell Chrissie all of that later when their own relationship was far more firmly established. For now, he mentally crossed his fingers behind his back and assured himself that he was doing the right thing. Smiling at her, he replied, 'Yes, so far as I know, they've always been extremely happy together.'

She had the reassurance she needed, so why did she feel that Guy was keeping something from her? Withholding something from her? Chrissie wondered.

'We *can't* go on like this,' Guy was telling her groaningly less than an hour later as they lay together on his bed, Guy's hand resting possessively and tenderly on her body as he kissed her gently in the aftermath of their passionate lovemaking. 'I wanted to keep you to myself for just a little while longer before we went public but...'

'What are you trying to say?' Chrissie asked him, but from the excited way her heart was racing, she suspected she already knew.

'We could fly to Amsterdam tomorrow,' Guy told her softly. 'I know a dealer there who specialises in antique jewellery, or if you'd prefer something more modern...'

Chrissie's heart leaped into her throat. 'An engagement ring, do you mean?' she whispered.

'An engagement ring and, more importantly, a wedding ring,' Guy affirmed throatily as he bent his head to kiss her.

'We *can't* get married just like that,' Chrissie protested, but the look in her eyes as they met Guy's revealed just how much she would like to. 'My parents...' she began. Guy nodded regretfully and agreed.

'My family will be just as bad. If we don't have a big formal wedding, there'll be no end to the sulks and looks of disapproval.'

'Marriage,' Chrissie said wonderingly, her heart in her eyes as she asked him huskily, 'Are you sure that that's what you want...that I'm what you want?'

'More sure than I've ever been of any other thing in my whole life,' Guy told her solemnly and meant it.

'We can talk about it properly tonight,' Chrissie promised, then reminded him, 'If I don't leave now,

I'm going to be late for my appointment with Jon Crighton.'

'Tonight,' Guy agreed. 'Tonight we'll make our real vows to one another, our real promises...our real plans. It'll be our last chance before we're swamped with offers of bridesmaids and wedding cakes.'

Chrissie laughed, leaned forward and then smiled up into his eyes as he drew her closer to him for one last, lingering kiss. She would remember this moment for ever, she promised herself. Remember the smell and feel of him, his warmth, their shared closeness, the almost physical presence of their shared love as it engulfed and cocooned them.

Yes, she would remember it for ever.

CHAPTER FIVE

CHRISSIE saw that Jon Crighton was frowning when he got up from behind his desk and walked across the room to stand in front of the window as he listened to what she had to say.

Jenny's husband had turned out to be a tall, blond-haired man in his fifties whose slight shyness couldn't really conceal the natural warmth of his personality, and now that she had met him she felt oddly reassured that Guy had spoken the truth when he said that Jon and Jenny had a good marriage.

'My parents, my mother, would like to have a list of Uncle Charles's debts, especially the names of those people he personally owed money to,' Chrissie told Jon, watching as his frown deepened.

'There's no legal responsibility on her part to meet such debts,' Jon began, but Chrissie shook her head and interrupted him.

'My mother and her brother were never close. I barely knew him and there was a problem, a quarrel, within the family, which meant... But still my mother feels very strongly that she doesn't want other people to suffer financially because they...because they trusted her brother perhaps unwisely. She has a very strong sense of family,' Chrissie explained quietly to Jon. 'And an equally strong sense of moral responsibility.' She took another deep breath and plunged on. 'She knows, *we* know, that her brother was not

82

always...honest in his dealings with other people.'
She paused and looked at Jon.

'No,' Jon agreed calmly. 'He wasn't, and I have to
be truthful, there are some people to whom he owed
money who will not be repaid out of what there is
left of an estate, who are financially in straitened circumstances themselves.' Jon paused, mentally reflecting on the wide differences that could exist between
two members of the same family. He was no stranger
to this state of affairs; he thought of his own brother
David and himself. 'Your mother need have no fears
that either she or her parents are remembered locally
with anything other than very great fondness and respect,' he told Chrissie gently, adding, 'Your grandmother, in particular, was very well known locally for
her generosity to a number of charities, both financially and through the voluntary work she did.'

'It's a family tradition my mother has continued,'
Chrissie informed him, going on to explain to him a
little of her parents' current way of life and the reasons why neither of them could be in Haslewich. 'To
be truthful, I'm rather glad that my mother didn't
come. The impression I've had from...from certain
people is that my uncle wasn't particularly well liked.'

'No, I'm afraid he wasn't,' Jon agreed after a telling but brief moment of hesitation. 'He was a drinker
and like all those who suffer from any kind of addiction, when he was in the grip of it, nothing and no
one else mattered.'

'I understand what you're saying,' Chrissie returned quietly. 'And my mother...' She stopped and
shook her head. It was obvious that Jon was well
aware of what the situation was and she was thankful

that there was no need for her to explain to him what manner of man her late uncle had been.

'There's no need for your mother to feel that her presence in Haslewich wouldn't be welcomed or that she will in any way be held responsible for her late brother's behaviour. There are very few families who can't count at least one black sheep amongst their number,' he added with a wry smile that warmed Chrissie's heart.

'I think my mother would *like* to come back. She often talks about the farm.'

Jon Crighton was an extremely likeable man, Chrissie reflected, all the more so because one could somehow sense that at heart he was basically a sincere and self-effacing person, one who would draw other people and their problems to him. He went on to tell her that he would do his best to expedite all the legal matters with regard to supplying her parents with a list of her late uncle's creditors.

'Although,' he added a touch hesitantly, 'from what I gather from my wife, it seems that you are not in any particular hurry to leave Haslewich.'

To her chagrin, Chrissie discovered that she was blushing as well as smiling as she made some inarticulate response to Jon's gentle teasing.

Half an hour later, their meeting concluded, Jon watched her as she walked across the town square. She was an attractive and pleasant self-possessed young woman and he could well understand why Guy Cooke should be 'smitten' with her as Jenny had claimed.

'Oh good, you're on your own.'

The sound of his wife's voice from the open doorway of his office had him turning round to welcome her. 'I thought when you phoned earlier you were going to be tied up for the day at Fitzburgh Place with the fair,' he commented.

'I was, but I decided to give myself a break, come home early and then perhaps go back later this evening. Is there any chance that you might be free to take me somewhere rather nice like the Grosvenor for afternoon tea?' she suggested.

'Mmm...' Jon pretended to give the matter some serious consideration before offering, 'I'm not so sure about the Grosvenor. We'd have to drive over to Chester and then back again, but there *is* this rather special little place I know where we could be all alone and where, if we're very lucky, we might be able to share rather more than afternoon tea.'

Jenny looked at her husband suspiciously. 'If you mean what I think you mean,' she began warningly, 'you're going to be out of luck. For one thing, I haven't been out shopping and we don't have a thing to eat other than last night's leftovers and for another...' She continued, overriding Jon's attempt to break in.

'I don't mind passing on the food,' he murmured.

'Jack and Joss will be at home.'

'Ah,' Jon sighed at this mention of the boys. Joss was his younger son and Jack was Jon's brother David's child. He had been living with Jon and Jenny since the breakup of his own parents' marriage.

Jack's married sister, Olivia, and her husband, Caspar, and their two young children lived close by and it had been Jack's own wish that he live with his aunt and uncle.

'Whom are you watching with such interest?' Jenny asked, walking over to the window to look through it. 'Ah…Guy's lady love. I'd forgotten she was coming to see you.'

'Mmm…she's nice. I liked her, and from what she's been telling me, her mother is nothing like her late brother. It seems that her mother and her uncle never really got on, but despite that, her parents apparently want to have a list of Charlie's main creditors so that they can pay off his debts.'

'That's very generous of them.'

'Very,' Jon agreed.

'But why has *she* come to Haslewich to deal with things and not her mother?'

'I rather suspect from what she didn't say that her mother, obviously knowing her late brother, feels that the residents of Haslewich might not make her very welcome, but as I pointed out to Chrissie, every family has its black sheep, and sometimes more than one of them, as we know all too well.'

Jenny looked up at him. 'I *do* wish David would get in touch with your father. It would mean so much to him, and apart from that card he sent at Christmas, he hasn't contacted Ben at all.'

'I know,' Jon agreed, placing his hand on his wife's shoulder and drawing her in against his body. 'Dad's Christmas card had a Spanish postmark, but David seems determined to keep his actual whereabouts a secret.'

'Perhaps it's for the best,' Jenny suggested, looking up at her husband. 'After all, if he *did* come back, what could he do? He couldn't come back to work here…not after…'

'No, he certainly couldn't do that,' Jon concurred sombrely.

'Do you still miss him?' Jenny asked gently. The brothers *were* twins, even if...

Jon shook his head. 'No, not really, not in a personal sense. But I do wish for Dad's sake that things could be different. He's been a changed man since David left.'

'He's getting old, Jon,' Jenny commiserated.

'Aren't we all?' Jon grimaced, thinking of the changes that the past few years had brought. Since that fateful night of the brothers' shared fiftieth birthday party and David's near fatal heart attack, both of them had become grandfathers, he through his son, Max, who was now married with two children and David through his daughter, Olivia, but whilst *he* saw his grandchildren regularly and enjoyed their company, he doubted that David even knew of his grandchildren's existence.

'Olivia was telling me the other day that Tiggy has decided that she wants to divorce David,' Jenny commented.

'Yes, I know,' Jon agreed. 'In fact, Olivia and I were discussing it only the other day. Tiggy's new man wants to marry her and he's pressing her to do something about ending her marriage to David.'

Jenny looked at her husband, unable to stop herself from asking, 'Do you...?' She bit her lip, wondering if it was wise to remind Jon that there had been a time when, if only fleetingly, *he* had been tempted to break his own marriage vows over his twin brother's wife, just as she had, oh so briefly, been tempted to respond to Guy's need for her.

But Jon, it seemed, had read her mind because he immediately shook his head and took hold of both her hands as he told her quietly, 'The only regret I have is that I was ever foolish enough to risk losing you,' he admitted truthfully.

'Oh, Jon,' Jenny whispered as she went into his arms and leaned her head against his chest. 'I do hope that everything works out for Guy with Chrissie. He's head over heels in love with her...'

'And she with him if the way she looked this afternoon when I mentioned his name is anything to go by,' Jon assured her.

'Well, she certainly looked as though she loved him when I saw them together, but...' Jenny nibbled at her bottom lip.

'But what?' Jon gave her a rueful look. 'Do I detect just a hint of the protective mother sheep anxious for her vulnerable little lamb there?' he asked her.

Jenny shook her head and grimaced. 'All right,' she agreed apologetically, 'perhaps I *am* being overly anxious and Guy is far too masculine to ever be called a lamb type but, well, they've known each other such a short time and if you'd seen the way Guy was looking at her...'

'You said yourself at Christmas that you'd like to see him married with children of his own.'

'Yes. I would, I do,' Jenny concurred. 'You're right.' She laughed. 'I admit it, I *am* being overprotective and Chrissie seems as head over heels in love with him as he is with her.'

She put her hand through Jon's and snuggled up to him, returning the loving look he was giving her as he looked down at her.

*   *   *

'Hello there...'

Chrissie gave a small start and then smiled as she realised that the woman addressing her in the street was Guy's sister.

She had another woman with her, some years younger than she was herself and who, Chrissie suspected from her rather strikingly handsome face and thick, dark curly hair, was probably another member of the family.

'I enjoyed meeting you last night,' Frances commented with another smile before turning to introduce her companion, explaining, 'Guy brought Chrissie over for dinner last night.' She looked at Chrissie. 'Natalie is another member of the Cooke clan.'

'Do you know Guy well?' Natalie asked abruptly, ignoring Chrissie's outstretched hand and frowning rather fiercely at her as she waited for a response.

Her glowering intensity made Chrissie feel uncomfortable and unsure of just how she ought to answer, but before she could say anything, Frances was replying for her, looking at Chrissie with teasing warmth as she informed Natalie, 'Not as well as Guy intends to make sure she *does* know him, if the way he was looking at her last night is anything to go by.'

'Oh, it's like that, is it?' Natalie responded disparagingly, flicking a disdainful and dismissive glance in Chrissie's direction. 'Well, Guy is always falling in love—and out of it even faster. He's a dreadful flirt.'

'Natalie,' Frances objected, frowning at her companion and giving Chrissie a rueful look.

'Well, it's the truth,' Natalie continued, ignoring the warning Frances was trying to give her. 'Guy's always been susceptible to a certain type of woman and, of course, we all know how he was over Jenny Crighton.'

'Natalie,' Frances protested rather more sharply.

'I'm not lying,' Natalie insisted with a scornful toss of her head. 'Guy can be a lovesick fool at times. Look, I've got to go,' she said, ignoring Chrissie completely as she bent to brush Frances's cheek with her lips and then turned on her heel to walk away.

'I'm sorry about that,' Frances apologised uncomfortably after she had gone. 'Natalie doesn't always realise…she's…' She glanced unhappily into Chrissie's pale, set face and sighed.

Natalie could be the limit at times. As a family, they were used to her disruptiveness and her acid remarks. She was and always had been the kind of person who enjoyed hurting and discomforting others. Frances tried to tell herself it was because at heart Natalie felt insecure herself rather than because she possessed a mean and spiteful nature, but sometimes Frances did wonder.

And, of course, it didn't help that the whole family knew that Natalie had had a bit of a thing about Guy for years. Not that he had ever been remotely interested in her in that way. She simply wasn't his type. Guy had a distinctly chivalrous, protective side to his nature that instinctively drew him towards the kind of femininely gentle woman whom he could take under his wing and protect. Even if she had been his type physically, which she wasn't, Natalie's personality was far too brash and abrasive ever to appeal to Guy. But family loyalty and the sheer complexity of the situation prevented Frances from explaining things to Chrissie. She would, however, have to go and alert

Guy as to what had happened as it was quite plain that Natalie's remarks had upset Chrissie.

'I'm not sure how long you're going to be staying in town,' she said gently to Chrissie now, 'but it's rather fortunate that I've bumped into you like this because I *was* planning to get in touch with you to ask you round for a meal. I don't know how much Guy has told you about our family, but it's rather a tradition for us that we all get together one Sunday in the month. Because so many of us work in the pub or catering trade in one way or another, getting time off together isn't always easy, so we take it in turns to host our monthly Sundays. It's my turn this month and we'd love it if you could join us.'

'Thank you, you're very kind,' Chrissie replied in a slightly stilted voice.

She wasn't so naïve as not to have been aware that Natalie had been slightly malicious in talking about Guy the way she had, but Chrissie had seen, too, how Frances had reacted to the other woman's comments and had sensed that there was just enough truth, specifically in what Natalie had said about Jenny Crighton, for Frances to feel uncomfortable.

Guy was bound to have had other relationships in his life, Chrissie realised, but *why* hadn't he been truthful and honest with her about his relationship with Jenny Crighton instead of concealing it from her? 'Guy is always falling in love—and out of—it,' Natalie had said scornfully.

Five minutes later, retracing her steps towards her late uncle's small house, she was forced to ask herself how much she really knew about Guy.

A stiff, chilly wind had risen whilst she was in Jon

Crighton's office and several ominous grey clouds were now obscuring the sun, warning her that she had been too trusting and optimistic in coming out wearing just a thin cotton dress. Just as she had been too trusting in believing Guy?

Chrissie looked a little apprehensively at her watch. Another hour and Guy would be here. The bright, sunny promise of the morning had given way to a cold, wet evening. The cottage, without the benefit of central heating, felt cold and smelt damp, and for the first time since she had arrived in Haslewich she was conscious of a feeling of alienation and loneliness.

It didn't help that her parents would now be well on their way on the first leg of their trip to Mexico and that she was unable to even pick up the phone and hear the comforting sound of a familiar and loving voice.

But surely she had all the comfort and love she needed here with Guy. *Guy*, the man whom only this morning she'd been making plans to spend the rest of her life with. *Guy*, the man who suddenly in the space of a brief conversation had become almost a stranger to her.

She was being silly, she warned herself. There was bound to be a simple explanation for Guy's omission in telling her about Jenny Crighton. All she had to do was to ask him for it.

Guy was just leaving the local delicatessen with the purchases he had made for his supper with Chrissie when he saw Jon and Jenny crossing the square.

'Mmm...you've been in Lawfords,' Jenny commented enviously when she saw what he was carrying. 'Lucky you, their food is wonderful but a little bit pricey when you've got two hungry teenage boys to feed. No need for me to ask whom *you're* planning to share your feast with,' she added teasingly.

'No need at all,' Guy agreed dryly.

'Chrissie seems a lovely girl, Guy,' Jenny remarked warmly. 'But I can understand why she feels a little bit wary about going public with the fact that Charlie was her uncle. Of course, the family virtually disowned him years ago, we all know that. Oh, and by the way, you'll never guess what. The police apparently suspect that there may be a woman involved with the gang who've been doing the break-ins locally.'

Jenny saw the way Guy was frowning and shook her head.

'It sounds odd, I know, but it seems it's often easier for a woman to get inside a target house and check to see what's there that's worth stealing. She then passes this information on to the rest of the gang.'

'Heavens, is that the time!' she exclaimed as the church clock chimed the hour. 'We'd better go. Enjoy your dinner party.'

Guy was still frowning as he watched Jon and Jenny walk away. Chrissie was Charlie Platt's *niece*? Then *why* hadn't she told him so? *Why* had she deliberately concealed the relationship from him and given him to believe that she was simply *acting* for the family, rather than being a closely related member of it?

He could remember quite vividly how, when he was a child, Charlie used to lie to him and pretend that he wanted to be his friend, that his malicious and cruel bullying of him had simply been a mistake. Guy could remember, too, how Charlie had taunted him when he had fallen for his lies and believed him. The wariness and cynicism, the hardness he had begun to develop as a means of protecting himself from the likes of Charlie Platt had stood him in good stead as an antiques dealer. It was a business where it paid to be cautious and a little bit suspicious at times, to thoroughly check the ownership of goods offered to him for sale rather than to automatically assume that the would-be seller had the right to dispose of them, but it had simply never occurred to him to be suspicious or wary where *Chrissie* was concerned.

He had taken her completely on trust, believed her every word utterly, and he had never even thought of questioning or doubting her. His response to her had been so immediate, so intense, so emotional, that it had left no room for logic or rational thinking.

But she had obviously not felt the same, had she? Otherwise it would never have occurred to her to withhold from him the fact that she was Charlie's niece.

To withhold from him. He grimaced to himself, his face suddenly bleak and cold.

Even now, he was *still* trying to make excuses for her. She hadn't simply *withheld* the truth from him; she had deliberately deceived him. There had been plenty of opportunity for her to tell him the truth, to explain to him just what her real relationship with Charlie was.

But her deceit seemed so out of character for her. One of the things that had struck him most forcibly about her had been her naturalness, her openness, her warmth, but quite plainly they were only illusory...manufactured.

As he crossed the square and headed for his own home, he tried to reason with himself that he was overreacting, that he was judging her, condemning her, without allowing her a fair hearing. There could, after all, be some perfectly logical explanation of *why* she hadn't told him the truth.

Such as? the more cynical side of his nature demanded harshly.

A simple case of forgetfulness. Oh, by the way, I forgot. Charlie Platt was actually my uncle.

He shook his head, mentally deriding himself and in the fashion of his teenage nieces and nephews adding a sardonic *Not*.

By the time he had returned to his house, the shock of Jenny's unintentional revelation was beginning to subside enough for him to pause and respond politely to Ruth's comments about the attractive display of flowers in his small front garden.

Ruth lived a few doors away from him and he knew her both via her charity work and through her relationship with Jenny.

She was an elegantly attractive woman who still bloomed with the joy of rediscovering and marrying the man she had originally fallen in love with as a young girl. And if these days her life and her world was a rather more cosmopolitan one than that of a small Cheshire country town, with six months of the year spent in America with her new husband and their daughter and family and six months back home in

Haslewich, she was still very much the extraordinarily warm and perceptive person she had always been.

'I can't take any credit for them,' Guy admitted in response to her comment about his garden. 'Unlike you, I'm afraid my fingers are not particularly green and I have to rely on Bernard to ensure my garden doesn't let the close down.'

Bernard Philips was yet another member of the extended Cooke clan, a second cousin of Guy's, who together with his two sons and his daughter had built up a local garden centre business—a business that Guy, in true entrepreneurial fashion, had yet another small investment in.

It was not for nothing that certain members of his family teasingly nicknamed him 'The Banker'.

He had a reputation amongst his family and friends, he knew, as a shrewd and astute businessman, and it had only been the previous Christmas that his sisters had been teasing him about the fact that he was too logical, too keen to weigh up the pros and cons to ever allow himself to fall deeply in love. And until he had met Chrissie, he had been inclined to share that belief.

Chrissie... Perhaps it would have been better if he had never met her, he decided savagely after he'd said goodbye to Ruth and let himself into his house.

Which was she really? The open, warm soul mate he had believed he had found, or someone very different?

Was *she* at fault for deceiving him or was *he* simply a fool for having deceived himself, for having credited her with virtues and attributes she simply didn't possess?

Had *he* imposed on her his own idealised version of her, lifting what was really merely an earthy lust into the realm of something more spiritual and divine?

Half an hour later, having abandoned his half-hearted preparations for their supper, he acknowledged that the only way he was going to discover the truth was by asking Chrissie outright why she had not told him about her relationship with Charlie Platt.

CHAPTER SIX

DESPITE the thorough cleaning she had given it, her late uncle's house still had that faintly musty smell she associated with neglect and decay, Chrissie acknowledged, wrinkling her nose slightly.

The old sheet she had thrown over the desk to protect it had slipped off, and as she went to replace it, she paused, studying the desk affectionately. She could well understand why her mother wanted to buy it from the estate.

It possessed a warmth and sturdiness that encouraged one to reach out and stroke the wood and Chrissie smiled a little to herself as she did so.

She was no expert but she doubted that the desk would prove to be very expensive. It would be her mother's birthday in two months' time and she was tempted to buy it herself and give it to her mother as a birthday present.

She was still smiling at the thought of her mother's pleasure when Guy knocked on the front door.

Quickly she went to let him in and was taken aback when she saw that he was frowning and that instead of moving to take her in his arms as she had been expecting, he actually seemed to move away from her as though he wanted to put some distance between them.

Natalie's contemptuous earlier comments ran through her brain and she hesitated uncertainly. Outside, the temperature had dropped and Chrissie felt a chill in the air inside the cottage. Shivering slightly, she turned to get her coat. The door to the small front sitting room was still open, and as she retrieved her coat from the hall chair where she had left it, she saw Guy freeze as he looked into the room.

'What is it…what's wrong?' she asked him anxiously.

'What's that desk doing here?' Guy demanded harshly.

Chrissie frowned as she heard the sharp accusatory note in his voice, her heart sinking.

'I'm waiting to get it valued. It belonged to…' She stopped and bit her lip. Guy was looking at her in a most peculiar way.

'Do go on,' he told her mock-gently. 'Or shall *I* say it for you? It belonged to Charlie Platt, better known locally as, at best, a con man and, at worst, a thief. A man who by no stretch of the imagination could ever legally or rightfully be the owner of *that* particular piece of furniture.'

'A con man!'

Chrissie went pale as she heard the pent-up fury in Guy's voice. She had known all along that he hadn't liked her uncle, had guessed it, sensed it, from all that he had not said about him rather than from what she'd heard, but the venom and bitterness she could now hear—see—in him seemed so totally out of character, so much the complete opposite from the tender, adoring lover who had left her only hours before that she could only stare at him in shocked bewilderment.

'But then, *you* probably know all this already, don't you, Chrissie? Which is why you've taken such good care to conceal this desk from me…just as you've also concealed from me the fact that Charlie Platt was your uncle.'

'No!' Chrissie protested.

'No? No what?' Guy demanded savagely. 'No, he wasn't your uncle?'

Chrissie bit her lip. She was in too much of a state of shock to speak or defend herself.

She had known, of course, that sooner or later she was going to have to tell Guy who she was. And if she was honest, she had perhaps put off telling him longer than she ought, but she had never dreamt he would react like this, *accuse* her like this. Look at her as though…as though he found her utterly and completely beneath his contempt, a creature so, so far beneath him that he could hardly even bear to look at her.

'I…I *was* going to tell you…I *wanted* to tell you,' she protested huskily, 'but—'

'Of course you did,' Guy interrupted with silky-smooth dislike.

'There hasn't been time…everything happened so quickly,' Chrissie told him doggedly, still trying to make him understand, to stop him before he ruined, destroyed, everything between them.

'Yes…too quickly for you to have time to get rid of this, I assume you mean,' Guy accused her grittily, giving a brief nod in the direction of the desk. 'I always knew Charlie wasn't too fussy about how he earned his drinking money, but I never realised he'd turned to fencing stolen property—'

'*Stolen*!' Chrissie exploded indignantly. 'That desk

wasn't stolen. It belonged to my great-grandmother, my—'

'*That* desk,' Guy cut across her curtly, his mouth compressing as he carefully spaced out every word, 'was *stolen* less than a fortnight ago from Queensmead. I'd know it anywhere, even without having seen the description the police have circulated. I appraised it for Ben Crighton—not that it has much commercial value. It's a copy of the French original,' he told her coldly, 'and as a copy isn't worth a tenth of the original.'

'You're lying,' Chrissie declared, her own shock and anguish giving way to an anger intense enough to match his own.

Just what was he trying to accuse her of doing? Just *what* was he trying to imply? She had her mother's word that the desk had belonged to *her* grandmother and she would take her mother's word against anyone's—*anyone's*—any day of the week.

'*I'm* lying…?' For a moment, the rage she could see in Guy's taut face and clenched fists was such that Chrissie automatically took a step back from him, her face going scarlet with mortification as he told her icily, 'I don't hit women. Not even a woman like you.'

A woman like her!

'How much more stolen stuff did he have stashed here, I wonder, and where is it now? I'm sure that's a question the police would be very interested in hearing the answer to.'

The police! Chrissie's heart gave a frightened bound but she wasn't going to let him panic or terrorise her. Why *should* she? She had done nothing wrong and neither, in this instance, had her late uncle. The desk belonged to their family and Guy had simply mistaken it for the one stolen from Queensmead. He had to have done.

As they confronted one another across the narrow width of the small hallway, Chrissie found it hard to believe that just a matter of hours ago they had been lying in one another's arms promising eternal fidelity and love, discussing the future they hoped to share together.

She wasn't sure if she wanted to laugh or cry. Possibly both. How *could* she have been such a fool? It was obvious to her now that Guy was dangerously volatile and untrustworthy where his relationships were concerned. How many other women had he treated...deceived...the way he had done her? Had he come here this evening looking for an excuse to quarrel with her, blame *her* for the fact that he had fallen out of love with her?

Love! He didn't begin to know the meaning of the word. But she did. Oh yes, she did, because, despite the pain he was now causing her, she knew perfectly well that if he was to turn to her, take her in his arms, beg her forgiveness, say it was all a mistake and it was just the shock of discovering she was Charlie's niece that had made him behave so cruelly, react so badly, she would want to accept his apology.

But one look at his face told her that he was going to do no such thing and rather than risk losing face by allowing him to see how much he was hurting her, how difficult she was finding it to distance and detach herself from him and all that they had shared, she drew herself up to her full height and told him quietly, 'I think, in the circumstances, you had better leave.'

'Do you know something?' Guy responded sarcastically. '*I* think you could be right. My God,' he added, shaking his head as he turned back towards the front door, 'you really had me fooled, do you know that? If Jenny hadn't let it slip that you were Charlie's niece—'

'I would have told you about that,' Chrissie said proudly. 'In fact, it was only because you were so antagonistic towards him that I—'

'You *lied* to me,' Guy interrupted coldly.

'Just as *you* lied to me when I asked you about Jenny,' Chrissie challenged him.

She wasn't going to let him have things all his own way, she decided. Why should she?

'I met your sister in town this afternoon. She had one of your relatives with her. It seems that you've got rather a reputation as an unreliable and fickle lover,' she told him with a bitter little smile. 'Pity I didn't hear about it *before* we met.'

He looked so angry that Chrissie's courage almost failed her. But why *should* she let him be the one making all the accusations?

Yes, she had been wrong not to tell him about Uncle Charles but at least she had not concealed important facts about her sexual and emotional history from him.

No wonder he had been such…such an experienced lover, she decided, summoning all the mental cynicism and self-protection she could whilst fighting to suppress the aching weight of her inner anguish and heartbreak.

'I don't know what you've heard or from whom,' Guy returned bleakly, 'nor do I really care. What I felt for Jenny was a private and personal thing and at no time did Jenny reciprocate my feelings or waver from her love for Jon.'

'Well, you would say that, wouldn't you?' Chrissie sneered with deliberately calculated nastiness.

'You bitch!' Guy snarled as he wrenched open the front door and stormed through it.

The cottage was already more than damp enough without her adding to its mildewy atmosphere with her tears, Chrissie remonstrated with herself well over an hour later when the now-silent tears of loss and pain were still trickling hopelessly down her face to betray her each time she thought she had them under control.

Instead, to keep her hands if not her mind occupied, she had spent the evening rescrubbing every inch of the small, old-fashioned kitchen and so much so that her hands now felt as raw and tender as her emotions.

How *could* she ever have been such a fool as to believe Guy when he told her that he loved her? She must have been bemused, bedevilled, besotted. There was no other logical explanation for what had happened—no *logical* explanation at all.

Of course, he hadn't loved her. How could he? He didn't know her. He had probably just been using her to ease the pain of his—according to him, she decided darkly—unrequited love for Jenny. No, of course he hadn't loved her. Just as *she* hadn't loved him. So then, if she hadn't loved him, why on earth was she behaving like a tragedy queen, wringing her hands and crying, yes, *crying* foolish tears into a silent house? She ought to be feeling grateful that she had discovered so quickly just what he was.

All those unbelievable lies he had told her about wanting to take her to Amsterdam to buy her an engagement ring. Yes, she was far, far better off without him, she decided.

After he left Chrissie, Guy didn't go straight home. How could he? For the first time since he had left his young manhood behind him, he knew what it was to feel the need to expel his pent-up emotions via some act of physical violence, albeit not against another human being and not even against himself. However, he admitted grimly, right now he could see a lot of virtue in being able to hit some inanimate object very hard. Very, very hard.

He frowned as he suddenly realised that his fast-paced walk through the town had inadvertently brought him to his old junior school—the scene of his long-ago childhood fear of Charlie Platt and the bullying and attempted blackmail Charlie had inflicted on him there.

'I *was* going to tell you,' Chrissie had cried defensively when he had confronted her with the truth. But why should he believe her, how could he believe her, especially after he had seen that damned desk? And *she* had had the effrontery to pretend that it belonged to her family.

There had been a moment when he had seen the look in her eyes, that had made him doubt... wonder...but then she had thrown that accusation at him about his supposed reputation and followed it up with that even more contemptuous comment about Jenny.

He stared across the empty playground, mentally reliving their quarrel. His anger had gone now, leaving him feeling flat and drained, empty and disillusioned.

He should have listened to that small warning voice that had urged him to be more cautious instead of... But the damage was done now. His love for Jenny had been a slow-growing, gentle emotion that he had lived with for a long time and one that he had come to realise was undoubtedly the result of being too much alone and of recognising in Jenny the type of woman who couldn't help but nurture and support others.

His love for Chrissie had hit him like a bolt out of the blue. It had been an overwhelming force. It had possessed a passion, an intensity, a recklessness that had made him step so far outside his normal character, that at times, when he was with her, he had barely recognised himself. His love for her had...

Had? His mouth twisted with cynical self-mockery as he turned away from the school and started to walk home.

Just who did he think he was kidding? Love... The kind of emotion he had for Chrissie couldn't be wiped out by a mere act of will, no matter how much his pride and self-respect might demand that it was.

Half an hour later when he walked into his comfortable kitchen, the first thing he saw was the supper he had prepared for Chrissie. Grimly he picked up the dishes of mouth-wateringly delicious epicurean delicacies and thrust the whole lot into the garbage.

The vintage bottle of wine he had bought to go with their meal was still on the table. He picked it up, glanced at the garbage and then looked ruefully at the bottle. He couldn't do it. It was too sacrilegious. He had opened the bottle and left the wine to breathe before going out. Absently he poured himself a glass.

It was good, but not even its warm mellowness could ease the harsh, gritty pain he was feeling. He emptied the glass and poured himself another. He had always prided himself on being a good judge of character but tonight he had had proof of just how poor his judgement actually was. He had been utterly and completely taken in by Chrissie.

His wineglass was empty. He frowned as he refilled it. It was pointless now to curse the fate that had brought them together. Better to curse his own folly in being deceived by it and by her. He looked blearily at the wine bottle, now three-quarters empty. There was no point in wasting what was left. Picking up the bottle and his glass, he headed for the stairs.

Guy was dreaming, drawing Chrissie closer to him as he savoured the familiar warmth of her body, frowning as he felt her tense and look back over her shoulder to where another man was watching them.

'Why are you looking at *him*?' he demanded jealously as he watched Charlie Platt smirking at him from the shadow of the school gates. 'You know who he is, don't you?'

'I have to go to him,' Chrissie was protesting as she pulled away from his embrace. Then somehow Charlie was standing next to them, towering over him as he had done when Guy was a little boy, grinning tauntingly at Guy as he took hold of Chrissie's arm.

'You didn't really think it was *you* she wanted, did you?' Charlie challenged, then he and Chrissie were walking away from him and he heard Charlie laughing and saying gloatingly to her, 'Look what I've got for you,' as he showed her the desk that for some reason had manifested itself on the pavement.

'No. You mustn't touch it,' Guy heard himself protest, but Chrissie only laughed.

'Of course I can touch it,' she told Guy. 'It's mine. Charlie gave it to me.'

'No,' Guy denied, the sound of his own raw denial bringing him abruptly out of his dream to sit bolt upright in bed, blinking in the darkness as he tried to shake away the disturbing emotions aroused by his dream.

'Chrissie feels a little bit wary about going public with the fact that Charlie was her uncle,' Jenny had informed him innocently.

'That desk wasn't stolen. It belonged to my great-grandmother,' Chrissie had told him boldly.

'The police suspect that there may be a woman involved with the gang,' Jenny had said.

Guy groaned and rolled over in bed, punching his pillow. Of course Chrissie couldn't be connected with the gang who had broken into Queensmead. He was convinced of it. But twenty-four hours ago he had been equally convinced that she was incapable of any kind of deception or deceit, hadn't he?

Wide awake now, he lay on his back and stared up at the ceiling. Ridiculously, given what he now knew

about her, his body, and not just his body but his
emotions, too, literally ached with yearning for her.

He had *never* felt like this about a woman before,
no, not even about Jenny. He had been right, then,
about one thing: Chrissie was destined to be the one
woman he would love. But he had sadly deluded himself about so many others, such as the fact that she
shared his feelings.

What was still a mystery to him was the way she
had allowed a relationship to develop between them
in the first place. Out of boredom? Simply as a means
of passing the time whilst she was in Haslewich?

He would have staked his life on the slight hesitation and sexual inexperience she had revealed being
genuine and on the belief that she simply wasn't the
type to play sexual games.

His head ached from the wine he had drunk and
his heart and his body ached even more from the bitter
brew Chrissie had given him.

Grimly he closed his eyes, reminding himself that
he was not a teenager and that he had responsibilities
and duties. Savagely he asked himself if he wanted
the whole county to know what a fool he had been.

Guy was just replacing the telephone receiver when
he heard his front doorbell ring. Despite the paraceta-
mol he had taken when he woke up, his head still
ached appallingly, but that didn't stop his heart giving
a short, savage jerk of expectation as he got up and
went to open the door. Only, of course, it wasn't
Chrissie standing on the other side of it. How could
it have been? That was over and if he had any sense
at all he would be thankful that it had ended before

he had had the chance to make even more of a fool of himself than he already had.

'Guy, are you all right?' Jenny asked in concern as he waved her in. 'You look dreadful.'

As he stood wincing in the bright sunlight, Guy suspected his expression gave her the answer.

'We've got a bit of a problem with one of the caterers for the fair,' Jenny explained as she followed him into the kitchen. 'I didn't want to disturb you too early. Is Chrissie...?'

'She's not here,' Guy told her abruptly, adding curtly as he kept his back to her, 'It's over between us.'

'Guy.' He could hear the shocked disbelief in Jenny's voice. 'Everyone quarrels,' she sympathized gently, 'and I'm sure—'

'This wasn't a lovers' spat, Jen,' he countered grimly. He turned round. 'Until you mentioned it yesterday, I had no idea that Chrissie was related to Charlie Platt. She'd led me to believe that she was simply acting for the family.'

Jenny frowned. 'Oh, Guy, I'm sorry. I shouldn't have said anything. I never meant...I just assumed you knew.'

'No. I *didn't* know,' Guy contradicted her heavily. 'She lied to me,' he burst out as he started to pace the kitchen, 'and she—'

'Guy, I can understand how shocked you must be...how hurt you must feel,' Jenny told him gently. 'I *know* you never particularly liked Charlie, but have you thought maybe that's *why* Chrissie felt that she couldn't tell you about the relationship?' she counselled him.

Guy looked out of the window. Would Jenny feel as charitably inclined towards Chrissie when she knew about the desk? Somehow he doubted it.

'It isn't just the fact that she kept me in the dark about her connection to Charlie,' he said stiffly. 'There's...there's something else....'

He paused whilst Jenny waited, obviously puzzled.

'Ben's desk is there,' he told Jenny, adding harshly, 'I saw it with my own eyes, Jen. There was no mistaking it. I valued the damn thing for Ben, for God's sake, and I told her so but she still kept claiming that it belonged to *her* family. She obviously knew it didn't belong to Charlie. She had to. For one thing...if you'd seen the rest of the junk he had and for another...'

'Perhaps she does genuinely believe it belonged to Charlie,' Jenny suggested uncertainly.

'*Why*...why *should* she think such a thing when I've already told her that it didn't! I've *told* her, moreover, just who it does belong to.'

'Oh dear,' Jenny commiserated. 'I'm so sorry, Guy. I just don't know what to say. She seemed so nice, so genuine. You two seemed so right for one another. Perhaps if you were to try to talk to her again?'

'What for?' Guy demanded harshly. 'So she could lie to me a *second* time.' He shook his head. 'Anyway, it's too late. I've rung the police to inform them about the desk. I had to, Jenny,' he added quietly when she said nothing. '*You* know that.'

'Yes. I know that,' Jenny agreed unhappily.

'They're calling round for me in half an hour. They want me to go with them to identify the desk.'

'Oh, Guy, I'm so sorry,' Jenny repeated.

'Nowhere near as sorry as I am,' he told her shortly.

They discussed the problem with the caterer and then Jenny announced that she had to leave.

'Jen, you'll keep it to Jon and yourself, won't you?' Guy asked her abruptly. 'What I said about the desk…? At least for now.'

'Yes, of course I will,' she promised him.

'It will all have to come out in the open soon enough. God knows what kind of fool I'm going to look, especially with the family.'

'There *could* be a rational explanation, Guy,' Jenny tried to comfort him, but Guy merely gave a harshly bitter laugh.

'Thanks, Jen. Nice try, but we both know the truth. There's no way that desk could ever have belonged to Chrissie's family. It's a one-off…unique. It was made to order, and while I don't want to be unkind, there is no way that a small-scale farmer like Chrissie's great-grandfather could have afforded, or I suspect, *wanted*, to commission a piece of furniture of that type.

'The only reason the Crightons had it made, according to Ben, was because *his* father felt he had been cheated of his rightful inheritance when the Chester branch of the family refused to hand over the original to him when his mother had promised him that on her death he should have it.'

'Mmm…well, Ben's memory *can* be rather selective when he wants it to be,' Jenny told Guy ruefully. 'As I understand it, there was never any question of Ben's father inheriting the original desk, which is actually one of a *pair* made in France for the twin daughters of the Chester family, and as far as I know, Ben's father had the desk copied more out of pique and a desire to thumb his nose at the Chester branch rather than because the desk should rightfully have been his.'

'A pair. That's interesting. Where are they now?'

'Well, Laurence has one and Henry has the other. They're very pretty…French and a world away from Ben's copy, although none of us would ever dare say as much to him.' Jenny laughed. 'You know how much rivalry Ben feels for the Chester side of the family, and in his eyes, of course, his father could do no wrong, even though from what Ruth's told me, her father was an extremely self-willed and autocratic man. Ben tends to see him through rather rose-tinted spectacles, though, I'm afraid.

'Give Chrissie another chance, Guy,' she advised him, touching his arm lightly.

'I can't, it's too late. Too much has been said and I doubt that she would even want me to. Much as I might be tempted, fool that I am,' he added with dry self-mockery.

Chrissie might not have imbibed the best part of a full bottle of red wine before going to bed, but she had slept just as badly as Guy and for much the same reasons.

It was too late now to regret not telling him the truth about her family connection with Charlie right from the very start. At least that way he could have rejected her there and then, she told herself miserably, instead of waiting until she had fallen deeply and irrevocably in love with him.

If he had *really* loved her, he would have *listened* to her, *let* her explain...*wanted* her to explain, but he hadn't, had he? It had seemed as though he was actually looking for an excuse to end their relationship. Was it because, as she had been warned, he had already fallen out of love with her?

As for his comments, his accusations, about her great-grandmother's desk...

She tensed as she heard the knock on the door, her hopes soaring against all logic and common sense and making it come as even more of a shock to see the police car parked outside the house and the stern-faced police officer standing on the doorstep with Guy standing equally cold-eyed to one side of him.

'Miss Oldham?' the police officer asked her, and when Chrissie nodded her head, he started to step forward, explaining, 'We understand that you have a desk here, which we have reason to believe could be stolen property.'

'Stolen property?' Chrissie darted a furiously indignant look at Guy, who was following the police officer into the hall. 'I do have a desk here,' she agreed with as much dignity as she could, 'but far from being stolen, it is...*was*, in fact, the property of my late great-grandmother.'

'I see. And do you have any proof of this ownership?' the policeman asked.

Of course she hadn't any proof apart from her mother's memories of the desk and her belief that her brother, Charles, had appropriated it at the time of their mother's death.

Unwilling for Guy to hear her being forced to admit that she couldn't prove ownership of the desk, she lowered her voice as she turned her back on him and replied quietly, 'No, I'm afraid I don't. Only my mother's description of it and her belief that it belonged to her family.'

'I see, and where could we get in touch with your mother, please, miss?'

Chrissie bit her lip. 'I'm afraid you can't, not at the moment. She and my father are away on a business trip. That's why I'm here...because she...they couldn't come.'

'So what you're saying is that at the moment there's no one to corroborate your claim to ownership of the desk?'

'No, I'm afraid there isn't,' Chrissie agreed as evenly as possible. She could feel Guy's attention on her but there was no way she was going to turn round and give him the satisfaction of seeing the shame and despair she knew were in her eyes.

'And your mother...your parents...when will they be available?'

Chrissie bit her lip again. 'Not for quite some time.'

'And you, Mr Cooke, you believe this desk belongs to Mr Ben Crighton?'

'I *know* it belongs to him, Officer,' Guy corrected crisply. 'I valued it myself for him only a few months ago, and as you know, it *was* listed as one of the items stolen when the house was broken into.'

The way both men were looking at her was beginning to make Chrissie feel not just uncomfortable but actually guilty, as well. But she had *nothing* to feel guilty about. At the worst, the *very* worst, her mother had made a mistake and the desk was not the one she remembered, despite the fact that she had been so certain, so positive, in the way she had described it to Chrissie.

'My mother grew up with this desk,' Chrissie announced shakily, 'but if she…if there *has* been a mistake…'

'A mistake?' Guy derided, causing Chrissie to flash him a look of bitter contempt.

'A mistake,' she repeated firmly. 'Then I know she'll be the first to say so,' she told the policeman slowly. 'Until then, all I can do or say is…' She paused, appalled to discover her eyes were filling with tears. Fiercely she blinked them away. The last thing she wanted to do was to break down in front of Guy and let him see how much he had hurt her, how vulnerable he had made her feel.

'Well, I think the best thing we can do now is to have the desk removed until it can be properly identified,' the police officer said diplomatically.

Chrissie gave him a grave-eyed smile as he thanked her for her assistance and turned to leave. Her stomach muscles tensed when she realised that Guy was deliberately hanging back and that he wasn't going to leave with him.

'I had to inform the police about the desk,' he told her quietly once they were alone.

'Yes, I'm sure you did,' Chrissie agreed emotionlessly. And then, before she could stop herself, she burst out passionately, 'I know you think I'm lying, but I'm *not* and neither is my mother. That desk belongs in the family.'

'You weren't so sure of that ten minutes ago,' Guy reminded her pithily.

'My mother would *never* lie,' Chrissie asserted with

quiet dignity, her face burning with hot colour as she saw the contemptuous look he was giving her. 'She wouldn't,' she protested heatedly. 'She's not...'

'She's not what?' Guy baited her. 'Not like you?'

Chrissie had had enough. Without thinking, she tried to lash out at him, but he reacted quickly, catching her wrist in mid-air and holding it pinioned behind her.

'My God, you really are a vixen, aren't you?' he breathed. 'Your Uncle Charlie would have been proud of you. Why didn't you tell the truth about him, Chrissie?'

For a moment she thought he genuinely wanted to know, but then just in time she recognised her own foolish weakness.

'If I *told* you, you wouldn't understand,' she informed him proudly.

'No, I dare say I wouldn't,' Guy agreed bitingly, 'but I *do* understand *this*.' Before she could stop him, he had pushed her back against the wall, and still holding her pinioned, he was plundering her mouth with a kiss of such raw savagery that its heat almost physically burned her mouth. Yet unbelievably she was actually responding to it *and* to him, letting him invade her mouth, her senses, her *self*, without even trying to raise the slightest pitiful defence against him. Where was her pride, her respect, her self-esteem and sense of self-preservation?

'I hate you,' she spat at him untruthfully when he finally released her. 'I *hate* you and I *never* want to see you again. *Never*. Do you understand?' But it was too late. Guy had already gone, loudly slamming the door behind him as he left so that the noise drowned out the protest she had made too late.

Outside in the street, Guy couldn't quite believe what he had done. He had never *ever* behaved towards a woman with such...such brutality before...or ever imagined that he might *want* to. Never guessed that he could want someone so much that he had to disguise and mask his need with the kind of macho display of faked anger that he had always despised.

He had *wanted* to kiss Chrissie...wanted to do far more than merely kiss her, he admitted with a groan. *Still* wanted to. Dear God, when was it all going to end...where was it all going to end?

CHAPTER SEVEN

'CHRISSIE...'

To her chagrin, Chrissie felt her eyes fill with tears she was unable to prevent from spilling over as she heard the gentle concern in Jon's voice.

It had been several weeks since her quarrel with Guy and the only comfort she could offer herself was that since she had now experienced the worst shock that life could possibly give her, things could only get better. But alas not yet. No, she was quite definitely not feeling anything like better yet.

She had arrived for her appointment with Jon ten minutes ago but had found it wholly impossible to concentrate on what he was saying to her about her late uncle's debts. Sorting through her uncle's possessions, finding a new valuer to assess them, and dealing with the assorted paperwork had taken longer than she, or her mother, had ever anticipated.

'I'm so sorry,' she apologised through her tears, accepting the box of tissues he proffered her. 'It's just...'

Jon, who had heard from Jenny what had happened, said nothing. Privately he found it extremely difficult to believe that Chrissie could have had anything to do with the theft.

'I suppose you've heard that the police are still investigating?' Chrissie commented when she had finally stemmed her tears. 'I'd thought about going back home to look in the family albums in the hope that there might be a photograph with the desk in it,' Chrissie admitted, giving a bitter little laugh. 'My mother was so sure,' she told Jon passionately. 'She said that her grandmother really treasured the desk, that she could remember watching her polishing it. She said she could actually remember her crying as she touched it, although she pretended she hadn't been when she saw my mother watching her.'

'Would it help if you were to return home?' Jon suggested gently. 'I could fax you with the details—'

'No,' Chrissie interrupted, shaking her head fiercely. 'If I did that, I would feel other people might think... I don't want anyone to think I'm trying to...escape or run away,' she finished quickly.

Jon gave her a small smile. 'I understand,' he told her simply.

When Chrissie left his office half an hour later, she was beginning to feel uncomfortably sick. She had skipped breakfast this morning and for the previous three mornings, as well, and now although she knew she ought to be hungry, for some reason the mere thought of food was beginning to make her feel extremely unwell. She felt light-headed, too, and oddly dizzy, so dizzy, in fact, that she had to stop walking and reach out to hold on to the railings separating the short cut she had taken through the environs of Haslewich's very grand Norman church from the graveyard that lay beyond it.

She felt most peculiar, Chrissie acknowledged, and she rather thought she ought to just stand where she was for a little while longer before trying to walk back to Uncle Charlie's house.

As she shook her head trying to clear the unfamiliar muzziness that seemed to have semi-paralysed the normally clear-thinking working of her brain, she realised to her consternation that she was standing only yards away from the elegant row of houses of which Guy's was one, but even *that* knowledge didn't give her the strength to move and, if anything, only made her feel worse. Hot tears began to press painfully on the back of her eyes as she fought to control the surge of painful emotions that overwhelmed her.

Ruth was feeling rather irritated with herself. She should have been in America with Grant right now. He had had to fly out there earlier in the week to attend some business meetings and she had planned to go with him, but almost at the last minute she had changed her mind, moved by guilt at the distressingly pathetic vulnerability Ben had displayed following the break-in at Queensmead.

'I *know* he can be stubborn and cantankerous,' she had explained to Grant as she snuggled up blissfully with him in bed. She was ruefully aware as she did so how very much out of character her delight in the physical proximity of her husband and her still-almost honeymoon enjoyment of the pleasures of simply knowing they were going to be sleeping together and that *she* was going to wake up with him there beside her in the morning might seem to those who had known her simply as the unmarried and rather strait-laced maiden aunt of the Crighton family. Indeed, she realised how disapproving some people might be of a woman her age actually enjoying herself in the physical, sexual and emotional sense by being as deeply in love with her husband as a young girl in her twenties. In truth, she herself sometimes wondered if her enjoyment of their new-found discovery of one another *was* quite appropriate in a woman of her mature years, but Grant assured her that it *was*, most certainly.

'But he is my brother,' she had emphasised firmly when Grant tried to kiss her. Then she added more seriously, 'I'm worried about him, Grant. He's aged so much since the break-in, become so vulnerable, and he's got this operation facing him, as well. *Would* you mind if I didn't come with you this time?'

'Of course I damn well mind,' Grant had responded gruffly, 'and of course I understand.'

Predictably, though, Ben was going through one of his awkward phases, refusing to see her or anyone else, so she might just as well have gone with Grant after all. She was missing him quite desperately already and he wasn't due back for another week. Ruth started to frown as something or *someone* on the other side of the walkway from her bedroom window caught her attention.

The poor girl, whoever she was, didn't look very well at all, she decided as she watched Chrissie cling to the railing for support. Concern etching her features, Ruth started to make her way downstairs.

'Hello there. I saw you from my upstairs window,' Ruth announced. 'You don't look very well. Why don't you come inside and sit down for a few minutes?'

Chrissie hadn't heard Ruth approach and so there was no way she could hide her tear-stained face from her. She tried to refuse her kind offer, but Ruth was already taking hold of her and gently but very firmly drawing her in the direction of her open front door.

Feeling too weak to argue or protest, Chrissie wanly allowed Ruth to direct her. She had always been very independent, stubbornly so, her mother had sometimes fondly protested. But, oddly, right now she was actually glad to have someone else taking control and making her decisions for her.

Ruth's house was a few doors down from Guy's, and like his, the hallway and the sitting room beyond it, which she ushered Chrissie into, was furnished with a happy mingling of old and new. Unlike Guy's, though, every polished surface held an obviously precious collection of photographs and family memorabilia. Chrissie tensed as she glanced at one and recognised Jenny and Jon Crighton standing side by side and laughing happily into the camera.

'My nephew, Jon, and his wife,' Ruth told Chrissie with a smile as she saw her looking at it.

'You're a Crighton?' Chrissie asked shakily.

'I was, but not any more,' Ruth answered. 'Do you know Jon and Jenny?'

Chrissie bit her lip. 'Sort of. Jon is acting for...for my mother in the estate of her late brother, Charles Platt,' she informed Ruth, defiantly lifting her head and looking her straight in the eye. 'I'm Chrissie Oldham,' she added with deliberate emphasis, 'and Charles Platt was my uncle. I appreciate that he didn't have a very good reputation locally and if you want me—'

Ruth didn't allow her to go any further.

'*All* of us have relatives, family members, who by choice we'd prefer not to have in our lives,' she told

Chrissie calmly, guessing what was coming and unconsciously echoing Jon's comment to Jenny. 'Every family has its black sheep,' she said. 'I can certainly think of a few within my own,' she added cheerfully. But although her comment was deliberately casual, her discreet study of Chrissie's ashen face and tensely nervous fingers wasn't.

She was surely far more distressed than having Charlie Platt as an uncle would warrant. She didn't strike Ruth as a theatrically over-emotional type, but the bleakness Ruth could see in her eyes was beginning to worry her almost as much as her obvious physical vulnerability.

Quickly Ruth came to a decision.

'I'm going to make us both a cup of tea and then you can tell me all about it,' she informed Chrissie with kind firmness.

It had been a long time since anyone, never mind a stranger, had spoken to Chrissie with such determined authority. She was, after all, an adult woman and very much in charge of her own life, or rather she had been. The events of the past few weeks had shown her just how woefully inadequate she actually was when it came to dealing with emotional pain and trauma. She was still, for instance, actually dreaming that Guy had changed his mind; that he regretted the breakup, that he took back all his hurtful remarks and accusations. A dream indeed. But thinking about it was enough to bring a fresh glitter of tears to her eyes whilst Ruth had gone to make the tea.

'Right,' Ruth commanded ten minutes later, having poured them both a cup of fragrantly scented tea. 'Now, let's see. Where were we? Ah yes... You had just told me that Charles Platt was your uncle. He was a rather unsavoury character, I'm afraid,' she told Chrissie briskly. 'But I'm sure you already know that. I knew his mother and indeed his grandmother and your mother, too, although she left Haslewich some time ago, didn't she?'

'Yes,' Chrissie replied. 'She and my father are away travelling on business at the moment, which is why—'

'You are here on their behalf,' Ruth supplied for her.

'Partially,' Chrissie agreed cautiously.

She looked at Ruth and gave a small inner shrug. What was the point in not telling her the truth? Her mother, she knew, would understand, and it would be a relief to get the whole thing off her chest and unburden herself to someone. Painfully Chrissie started to speak.

'Oh dear,' Ruth sympathised when Chrissie eventually finished.

Ruth knew the desk Chrissie had referred to, of course. Her brother, Ben, was particularly attached to it because it had been one of the first pieces of furniture brought into their home by their father when he originally moved into Queensmead, but Ruth guessed that it wasn't so much the true ownership of a mere piece of wood, no matter how pretty, that was causing Chrissie so much distress.

'Have you tried to talk to Guy...explain?' she asked gently.

Chrissie shook her head. 'What's the point? He's already made his own judgement and anyway... They always say you should never put too much trust in passionately intense emotions, don't they, especially when...?' Chrissie took a sip of her tea and abruptly went pale. 'I'm sorry,' she gasped. 'I don't know what's wrong with me. It must be all the stress but I just keep feeling so sick. It can't be anything I've eaten because the mere thought of food makes me feel so horribly ill. I don't understand it. I'm normally so healthy.'

Ruth studied her thoughtfully. She had her own opinion of what could and could not make an otherwise patently healthy young woman unable to tolerate the thought of food and experience unfamiliar nausea. She had, after all, gone through the same experience herself, and as if that wasn't enough, the charity she had helped set up and still ran to provide emotional and practical support and care for single pregnant women had taught her to recognise perhaps earlier than most the tell-tale signs that suggested a woman might be pregnant.

'I don't want to interfere,' she began carefully, 'but...'

Ruth believed in plain speaking and being truthful and so she said quite simply, 'I may be way off course, but has it occurred to you that you might be pregnant?'

'No!' Chrissie gasped but even as she made the denial she knew that Ruth could well be right.

Was it really less than a couple of hours ago that she had been telling herself that she had faced the worst that life could possibly throw at her? Now, after listening to Ruth, she knew that she had been wrong. There could be worse. There *was* worse. Pregnant and with Guy's baby. How *could* this have happened to her?

Did she really need to ask herself that? After the passion and intensity with which she and Guy had made love, the wonder would have been in her not conceiving.

'I'm afraid I've given you a shock,' Ruth said gently, adding, 'I do know what it's like. I've been there myself.' She smiled as she saw Chrissie's disbelieving look. 'It was a long time ago, of course, and in a completely different climate. I felt I had to give my baby up for adoption.'

'Oh no, how awful,' Chrissie protested, unwittingly betraying to Ruth that already, even though *she* didn't know, Chrissie was going to be a fiercely protective and caring mother.

'Well, yes, it was, but I was lucky. Life gave me a second chance and my daughter...our daughter, is now very much a part of my and Grant's life,' she acknowledged. 'I know all this must be a shock for you, but you *are* going to have to tell Guy, you know.'

'No.' Chrissie's response was emphatic. 'It's nothing to do with him...and besides, he wouldn't want to know anyway.'

Ruth's eyebrows rose. 'Are you sure about that?' she queried. 'I *know* Guy, have known him ever since he was a little boy, and I think you'll find that he'll take his responsibilities towards his child *very* seriously.'

'But the baby wasn't planned. It was an *accident*,' Chrissie started to tell her. 'I don't need his help...or his sense of responsibility. I can manage on my own. This is *my* baby.'

Ruth listened sympathetically. How well she recognised *that* stubborn female pride and how well she recognised, too, all the heartache that went with it, not just for Chrissie, but for her child, as well, but wisely she only advised Chrissie, saying, 'We have a very good medical centre here in town with a doctor who specialises in gynaecological matters. It might be wise to make an appointment.'

'Yes, thank you, I will,' Chrissie affirmed stiffly, accepting the slip of paper Ruth handed her once she had written the doctor's name and address down on it.

Half an hour later, having given in to Ruth's persuasion to eat some dry toast and have a fresh cup of tea, she stepped a little shakily through Ruth's front door and out into the street, having thanked her not just for her hospitality but for her kindness, as well. Pregnant with Guy's baby. She might not want to believe it, but instinctively she knew that it was true.

Now what was she going to do? What was she going to tell her parents who, although broad-minded and very loving, were bound to be a little disconcerted to discover that they were soon to be grandparents. Wearily Chrissie closed her eyes, reminding herself that other women with far less supportive parents and fewer earning skills than her somehow managed and so would she.

Guy had had an extremely frustrating day. Lord Astlegh's bailiff had apparently caught one of the catering staff for the fair wandering through a part of the house that was quite definitely off limits. She in turn had claimed that she had simply lost her way and had waxed highly indignant over the bailiff's treatment of her.

'Making out like I was some kind of thief,' she had complained to Guy. 'Just who does he think he is?'

With the fair officially opening in the morning, this kind of complication was the last thing Guy needed, especially when—

He braked hard as he suddenly saw Chrissie emerging from a side street into the road he was driving along. Her head was down and she looked tired and defeated. He had an overwhelming urge to get out of the car and rush over to her to take her in his arms. These few weeks when he had avoided seeing her had been the longest of his life. God, *why* had he had to see that damned desk?

If he hadn't… *Yes*, he had been angry…hurt in many ways, that she had omitted telling him that Charlie was her uncle, but as she had so promptly reminded him, *he* had kept things about his own life from her, as well. Now that he had calmed down, he could appreciate, as Jenny had pointed out to him, that Chrissie had not told him that she was related to Charlie simply because she had been reluctant to create any kind of barrier between them.

'Give Chrissie another chance, Guy,' Jenny had advised him several weeks before. Her words now echoed in his mind.

Head down, Chrissie turned the corner without having seen him. The lights changed. Guy drove through them and then on impulse indicated left to follow

Chrissie. He stopped the car, ignoring the yellow line he was parked on, and loped down the street after her.

As she heard the sound of someone running behind her, Chrissie instinctively came to a halt and turned round, her expression betraying her shock as she realised who it was.

'Guy,' she breathed, unable to stop herself from reacting to his presence.

'Chrissie, are you all right?' Guy asked, frowning as he saw how pale and fragile she was looking.

'Of course I'm all right,' she snapped, starting to turn away from him, suddenly mindful of the pitfalls of her situation, but as she moved away, Guy reached out towards her, accidentally jolting her arm so that she dropped the piece of paper Ruth had given her that she still was holding in her hand.

Immediately she bent down to retrieve it, but Guy moved faster, picking it up and frowning as he recognised the name and address of one of their local doctors.

'If you're not ill, then what are you doing with Dr Jardine's name and address?' he questioned her tersely. 'You certainly don't *look* well.'

'I said I'm perfectly all right,' Chrissie lied through gritted teeth, 'and if you would just give me that back…'

Dr Jardine. Guy's frown deepened. He knew she was one of the doctors at the local practice, and although she was not his own doctor, for some reason the name was starting to ring a bell. Dr Jardine…

He was just about to hand the slip of paper back to Chrissie when he suddenly realised just why the name was so familiar. Dr Jardine was the doctor one of his sisters had seen when she was first having trouble conceiving. Dr Jardine was the practice's gynaecological specialist. *Gynaecological* specialist... *Why* did Chrissie need to see a gynaecologist? What was wrong? She looked so pale, so drawn, so hunted and haunted almost, heartachingly proud at the same time, her hand crossed defensively across her body as though in protection of...

'You're pregnant!' He said the words almost instinctively, intuitively, without pausing to analyse his thoughts before giving voice to them, but he knew the moment he saw Chrissie's face that he was right.

A flash-flood of complex emotions swamped him— shock, pain, joy, anger, pride and love...most of all love.

Chrissie looked away from Guy, compressing her lips, her heart sinking.

'Chrissie,' she heard Guy demanding urgently.

'I don't have anything to say,' Chrissie responded with shaky hauteur.

'So you *are* pregnant,' Guy breathed, 'with *my* baby...*my* child....'

'No,' Chrissie denied vehemently, spurred into action by his words. '*This* baby, if there *is* a baby, has *nothing* whatsoever to do with *you*. This baby is *mine* and only *mine*.'

'I doubt a court of law would take that view,' Guy challenged her harshly, too caught up in emotion to be cautious. He had never had any particular cravings for children, fatherhood—even though he had always got on well enough with his nephews and nieces, so why did he have this intense and atavistic sense of pride, of involvement...of possession almost immediately he discovered that Chrissie was carrying his child?

Chrissie stared at him.

'A court of law?' she protested. 'But—'

'A father has rights,' Guy informed her.

A *father*. Chrissie opened her mouth and then closed it again before declaring bitterly, 'I doubt fatherhood was very much on your mind when you...when I...when we...'

'Was motherhood on yours?' Guy challenged her.

There wasn't anything that Chrissie could say.

'We need to talk,' Guy said tersely, but Chrissie shook her head.

'Leave me alone, Guy,' she told him bitingly, turning her back on him and starting to walk swiftly down the street.

Angrily Guy began to follow her, catching up with her and taking hold of her arm to pull her round to face him.

'Let go of me,' Chrissie demanded furiously.

'Not so long ago you were begging me never to let you go,' Guy reminded her mercilessly.

Chrissie flushed hotly but managed to fight back, telling him cuttingly, 'And you were telling me that you loved me, but we both know...'

She paused and she could feel Guy's grip on her arm tighten slightly as he grated, 'We both know what, Chrissie?'

Chrissie shook her head. She felt tired and weak and cross with herself for wasting her fragile strength on arguing with Guy when her baby needed it so much more.

'My car's just round the corner. I'll take you

home,' Guy commanded grimly. 'Don't argue with me, Chrissie. You look as though you're about to collapse.'

She *felt* it, too, Chrissie acknowledged whilst she mentally berated herself for her weakness in allowing him to dictate her actions to her.

'When did you find out…about the baby?' Guy asked curtly once they were in the car.

'Does it matter?' Chrissie responded wearily, unwilling to tell him that she would probably still be in ignorance about her impending motherhood even now if Ruth hadn't enlightened her.

She closed her eyes. She really did feel quite unwell, and then she opened them again abruptly. This wasn't the way to her uncle's cottage. It wasn't the way to anywhere *she* knew at all.

'Where are you going? Stop the car at once. I want to get out,' she demanded furiously, reaching for the door handle only to discover that Guy had activated the central locking system.

'What are you doing? You have no right to do this!' she cried out. 'You—'

'I have my right as a father to protect the health of my unborn child,' Guy returned determinedly.

Chrissie couldn't find the words to respond. *His* right as a *father*.

She really did feel unwell; the motion of the car wasn't agreeing with her at all.

'Guy, I think I'm going to be sick,' she announced in a small voice.

'Right now?'

Chrissie nodded her head slowly.

Guy showed commendable promptitude and dexterity in stopping the car so swiftly and in refusing to display any male annoyance or distaste she might have expected in her nauseous condition, she decided ten minutes later when she was beginning to feel a little better.

'I want to go home,' she told him plaintively.

'You *need* to go somewhere where you can be looked after,' Guy responded dryly, 'and *that* is exactly where I am taking you. Come on....'

As he led her back to the car, Chrissie told herself that she was a fool for not taking her chance to escape from him whilst she had it, not, she suspected, that he would have let her get very far and she certainly didn't feel well enough physically to even *try* to outrun him.

As they got back in the car and he started the engine, she realised that he was driving away from the town. 'Where are we going?' she demanded again, uncertainly.

'I've just told you,' Guy responded calmly. 'Somewhere you and *our* baby will be looked after.'

Our baby... She wanted to protest that *her* baby had nothing whatsoever to do with him but she was too drained to make the effort. They were in the country now, driving down narrow lanes bounded by high hedges, and then Guy was turning off the main road and into a narrow dirt track, through a farm gate and towards the farm itself.

Chrissie's eyes widened as she saw it. Unable to stop herself, she turned to Guy and exclaimed feebly, 'This was my grandparents' farm....'

'Yes,' Guy affirmed. 'My sister and her husband bought it last year,' he went on to explain. 'It isn't a working farm any more. All the land had been sold off and all that was left was a couple of paddocks. My sister teaches disabled children to ride and so they needed the land for the ponies.'

'Your sister… How many have you got?' she asked him faintly.

'Five,' Guy told her dryly.

'Five!'

'You'll like her.'

'But you can't drive up and expect her… She won't—'

'She can and she will,' Guy corrected her, refraining from adding that he had helped his sister and her husband buy the house with an interest-free loan or that even apart from that act of generosity he knew that his sister with her generous heart would never turn away someone in need.

'Is that her?' Chrissie asked nervously as she saw the tall, dark-haired woman emerging from the front door of the farmhouse as they drove up.

'That's her,' Guy confirmed laconically.

As Guy stopped the car, she came running towards it and immediately Chrissie could see the family resemblance between them. They shared the same strong bone structure and dark hair, and despite the fact that she was obviously in her early fifties, Guy's sister still had an enviably slim and fit-looking body.

'Guy,' she exclaimed fondly as he opened the car door. 'What a lovely surprise. Oh, and you've brought someone with you, as well. You must be Chrissie.' She smiled as Chrissie looked uncertainly at her. 'I've heard about you from Frances.'

'Mmm…well, there's something that Frances *won't*

have told you,' Guy began, but Chrissie placed her hand on his arm, pleading with her eyes for him not to say any more.

'Chrissie and I are not exactly the best of friends at the moment,' he told his sister calmly, 'as I'm sure she'll lose no time in telling you. But right now, she isn't feeling very well. She's been living in that wretched hovel of a cottage that Charlie Platt used to own. The walls are running with damp and I've never been convinced that the old cesspit those cottages were built over was ever sealed off properly.'

'Mmm...it always used to smell rather odd down there on hot summer days,' his sister mused whilst Chrissie listened to them in growing anxiety.

The cottages were old enough to have been built in the days when jerry-builders had thrown up houses as cheaply as they could and she herself had been aware of an unpleasant mustiness about the air in the cottage, which she had previously put down to the damp. But supposing it was not. Supposing it was something more sinister...more dangerous and potentially harmful not just for her but for her baby, as well.

'You *do* look pale,' Guy's sister sympathised. 'Come inside and sit down. My name is Laura, by the way. Rick, my husband, is away at the moment trying to buy more ponies.'

'Guy said you taught disabled children to ride,' Chrissie commented as she walked to the house, flanked on one side by Laura and on the other by Guy.

'Yes, I do, and we desperately need some more, but it isn't easy to find the right kind of mount.'

As Laura opened the front door, Chrissie hesitated, looking round at her surroundings.

'Chrissie's grandparents used to own the farm,' Guy explained to his sister.

'Oh…' Laura frowned and then exclaimed, 'But that means—'

'That I'm a Platt,' Chrissie supplied with a tight smile. 'Well, yes, actually my mother *was* a Platt. Charlie was her brother,' she added, holding her head up high, her chin jutting out firmly as she dared either of them to make a critical comment.

'Oh yes,' Laura remarked, but instead of looking disapproving, Laura's face lightened in a warm smile.

'Yes, of course,' she agreed. 'I remember your mother from school. She was completely different from Charlie, very quiet and studious.'

'Yes, she was, she still is,' Chrissie acknowledged, quietly refusing to give in to the temptation to look at Guy to see how he was reacting to this confirmation of her mother's character.

'Look after her for me,' Guy told his sister half an hour later when she saw him out to his car, leaving Chrissie in the house.

She raised a querying eyebrow, but when Guy simply shook his head, she knew better than to press for an explanation.

It was obvious that they had quarrelled and equally obvious, too, that Chrissie was both unwell and unhappy, and Laura was simply not the kind to pry into other people's unhappiness or to demand confidences, but the white-faced, hollow-eyed young woman who had accompanied her equally grim-faced brother this afternoon bore no resemblance whatsoever to the couple Frances had described as being practically incandescent with love for one another.

As Guy drove away, she retraced her steps to the farmhouse. She found her visitor where she had left her, staring out of the sitting-room window at the farm land beyond.

'I'm sorry that Guy has dumped me on you like this,' Chrissie apologised awkwardly to Laura. 'If I could just call a taxi, I'll take myself off your hands.'

'It's more than my life's worth to let you do such a thing,' Laura countered humorously, adding more seriously, 'and besides, no matter how much we as women might quarrel with Guy's absurdly male high-handed behaviour, it *is* rather obvious that you aren't very well. We have plenty of room here, and in all honesty, I get lonely when my husband is away. You would be doing me a favour if you did stay for a few days. Guy's right about there being something polluted in the atmosphere in those cottages,' she remarked, shaking her head. 'I had a friend who lived in one and she was always ill.'

'I'm not ill,' Chrissie told her quietly. 'I think I'm pregnant. You must be shocked,' she added when Laura made no comment. 'I hadn't intended to tell you, but—'

'No, I'm not shocked,' Laura interrupted her, 'just rather envious. Rick and I have never been able to have children,' she explained, 'Of course, I'm too old now and well past the sharp unbearableness of the pain it used to cause me. My work has helped me with that and time.... Is the baby the cause of the problem you and Guy...?'

'No...not as such,' Chrissie replied, shaking her

head. 'Although…' She stopped. Perhaps now was not the time to tell Guy's sister that she suspected it could be a problem later if Guy insisted on claiming his rights as a father as he had already threatened he would. 'No, the problem is that…' She took a deep breath before continuing. 'The problem is that we both rushed into a relationship without knowing enough about one another,' she said sadly.

'And now that you do, what you thought was love has turned out to be…not love…?' Laura guessed.

Chrissie gave her a painful smile and told her wryly, 'I *wish*. I'd rather not talk about it if you don't mind,' she said tiredly.

'*I* don't mind in the least,' Laura assured her. 'I'll take you upstairs and show you where everything is, and then perhaps later when you're feeling a little more rested, we can drive into town and collect your things.'

CHAPTER EIGHT

'I THOUGHT if you were feeling up to it, we might drive over to Fitzburgh Place this morning,' Laura commented.

'Why?' Chrissie demanded suspiciously.

'It was the official opening of the Antiques Fair yesterday, and I rather thought it might be fun to rifle through a few bric-a-brac stalls,' Laura said encouragingly.

'Yes, it would,' Chrissie replied truthfully.

She had been staying with Laura for two days now and had to admit that she couldn't have had a better hostess. They were both on the same wavelength, sharing a rather dry sense of humour. Laura supplied the relaxed and unselfconscious mothering that Chrissie knew she needed at the moment and in other circumstances she recognised that in Laura she would have found a friend she would want to keep for life. But Laura was Guy's sister.

'No ulterior motives,' she challenged her.

'Not a single one,' Laura promised, adding, 'Guy *will* be there, of course, and if you feel you'd rather not go...'

Chrissie glanced through the kitchen window. It was a bright, sunny morning. She had woken up today without feeling sick and why should she deny herself and Laura a treat just because Guy was going to be there? Jon had almost completed the work on her late uncle's estate. It wouldn't be long before she would be able to return to her own life and, once there, she need never have to see Guy again.

'No, it'll be a nice outing,' she agreed, 'but if you're harbouring any plans for staging a reconciliation...' she warned darkly.

'You're adults, not children,' Laura responded calmly as Chrissie got up and started to clear away their breakfast dishes.

'Yes, we are.' Chrissie wondered as she watched Laura start loading the dishes into the dishwasher why the knowledge that Laura *wasn't* planning to try to bring her and Guy back together should leave her feeling so flat.

Surely she didn't *want* him back? After what he had said...after the accusations he had made? He had proved only too clearly that she was really better off without him in her life...in *their* lives.

But he *was* her baby's father. Comfortingly she touched her still-flat stomach as though to reassure the life growing within it that *she* would give it all the parenting it needed; that *she* would give it all the love it needed.

'Are you all right?' Laura asked her, frowning.

'Yes, yes, I'm fine,' Chrissie responded.

The previous day, she had seen the doctor who had cheerfully announced that so far as she could see, Chrissie was a perfectly healthy mother-to-be, if a somewhat nauseously inclined one.

'We generally find it stops around three to four months,' she had consoled Chrissie, laughing when Chrissie's face had dropped.

'Four months...?' she had wailed.

'I prefer not to prescribe antinausea drugs,' the doctor had added, 'unless the mother-to-be is so ill that it is beginning to affect the baby's growth. Have you tried a couple of dry biscuits in the morning when you wake up?'

Laura, too, had recommended the same remedy, explaining that although she had no personal experience of its efficacy, both her sisters who had suffered from the same problem had sworn by it.

'We could take a picnic lunch,' Laura was telling her now. 'As you'll have already seen the grounds are really something special, but I suspect Guy won't be too pleased with me if he learns that I've dragged you all round them.'

'Guy has absolutely no input into what I choose to do,' Chrissie informed her determinedly but either Laura hadn't heard her or she was choosing not to hear her, Chrissie recognised as the other woman busily wiped down the worktop before setting the dishwasher in motion.

'Guy *is* concerned about you,' she told Chrissie half an hour later as she drove them both to their destination. 'He telephones at least twice a day asking how you are.'

Chrissie averted her face before saying brusquely, 'He's not concerned about me. It's the baby he's worrying about. This is my baby, Laura,' she declared fiercely. 'It has nothing to do with Guy.'

'Apart from the fact that he is its father,' Laura reminded her.

Chrissie sighed. They had been over this argument several times during the past couple of days, and whilst Laura had in no way attempted to press Guy's claim, neither had she offered Chrissie the comfort of taking her side.

'Most men in his position would be only too glad to be told they had no responsibility,' Chrissie fretted.

'Some would, I agree,' Laura replied. 'But Guy simply isn't like that. He's always been extremely responsible.'

'But not responsible enough to check before he told me that he'd fallen in love with me that he really meant it,' Chrissie couldn't help retorting.

She bit her lip when Laura made no response. She hadn't intended to say what she had but sometimes the hurt of what Guy had done to her was just too much for her to bear.

'In fact, given his reputation, I'm only surprised that this hasn't happened to him before,' she muttered bitterly.

Now she had got Laura's attention and she could see the frowning lack of comprehension in the other woman's eyes as she unexpectedly brought the car to a halt at the side of the country lane they were travelling and demanded shortly, 'What on earth are you talking about, Chrissie? *What* reputation?'

Chrissie swallowed, dismayed to see the unexpectedly stern expression on Laura's face. It made her look disconcertingly similar to the way Chrissie could remember her mother looking at her over some childhood misdemeanour.

'I...er...Natalie mentioned it...' She found herself almost stammering as Laura continued to regard her with frowning concentration.

'Natalie,' Laura scoffed dismissively. 'That woman is a troublemaker who wouldn't recognise the truth if it walked past her in the street. Besides which Natalie has always been rather...possessive where Guy is concerned, completely without reason, and over the years I suspect she's been rather clever at manipulating certain situations to her own advantage. I can assure you, Chrissie, that Guy has *never* had the kind of reputation you're talking about. He has had women...friends, of course, relationships, but...'

She paused, shaking her head. 'This is an issue you should really be discussing with Guy, not me. I must confess I'm rather surprised at you, though, Chrissie,' she added, much to Chrissie's discomfort. 'I had thought you far too sensible and intelligent to be taken in by the spiteful comments of an obviously jealous woman.'

Chrissie gave a small shrug. 'It isn't important anyway,' she fibbed.

'Have the police been back to you yet regarding ownership of the desk?' Laura enquired as she restarted the car, changing the subject.

Chrissie shook her head. 'No, they say they want to wait until my parents return so that they can interview my mother. After all, she hasn't actually seen it yet and until she does...'

'When she and your father come to Haslewich, they'd be more than welcome to stay at the farm,' Laura told her. 'As you know, we've got the space and since this *was* your mother's childhood home...'

Chrissie was touched by the generous offer.

'I'll pass your invitation on to her,' she assured Laura. 'I know she'll be worried about coming.' She hesitated. 'She's also very sensitive about the reputation that her brother had in the town and—'

'Good heavens, no one will hold that against her, or judge her because of it,' Laura informed Chrissie firmly.

Chrissie bit her lip but couldn't prevent herself from saying quietly, 'Guy held it against me.' She heard Laura sigh.

'I don't know if I should tell you this,' Laura began quietly, 'but Guy had a very specific reason for not liking your uncle.'

Chrissie listened, horrified, as Laura went on to tell her about Charles's bullying of the not-so-robust little boy that Guy once was.

'That kind of thing can leave scars, especially for a man like Guy. He would never use his own physical strength against anyone else, he simply isn't like that. But I suspect that there's a macho instinct in every man that makes it hard for him to admit that another male has caused them to feel fear or physical pain. In their eyes it demeans them as a man. Guy was always scrupulous about not doing anything to take revenge for the way Charlie treated him when he was young. However, deep down inside himself, I think a part of him still carries what he sees as the humiliation of allowing Charlie to bully him, of not being able to stand up for himself and defend himself. Am I making any sense?' she asked Chrissie quietly. 'Or...'

'Yes,' Chrissie told her huskily, her eyes filling with tears. She could hardly bear the mental images Laura had so poignantly drawn for her and in her mind's eye she could clearly see the small, pale, perhaps even fragile-looking boy being tormented by his much bulkier and bigger tormentor and, yes, she could understand, too, what Laura meant when she said that

Guy might still carry a sense of humiliation because of what had happened. 'Why didn't he *tell* me…say something?' she asked Laura.

Laura's eyebrows rose. 'Do you really need to ask?' she returned dryly. 'He's a man.'

Chrissie sighed in acknowledgement of her comment.

Although Guy had shown Chrissie round the site of the Antiques Fair, what she had seen then had not prepared her for the scene that met her eyes when, after parking the car, she and Laura turned the corner into the stable yard.

It was like being transported back to an earlier and more robust century, Chrissie recognised, as all her senses were assailed by the sights, sounds and smells of a Victorian fair in progress.

Street musicians in costume played cheerful tunes; acrobats and a clever pickpocket were entertaining the crowd with their antics; on a stage elevated safely above the visitors, a fire-eater performed feats of daring. A pieman sang out his wares whilst a very convincing Gypsy woman with two highly enthusiastic children at her side, all in traditional costume and all, Chrissie suspected from their features, members of Guy's extended family, 'hawkcd' lucky pieces of heather, which Chrissie realised they were actually giving away.

Everything that could be done to create the authentic flavour of a bygone age *had* been done and Chrissie could only stand and marvel at the colourful and picturesque sight in front. 'Is *Guy* responsible for all of this…?' she asked Laura wonderingly.

'I'm afraid so,' Laura responded dryly. 'He loves it, you know. Oh, he pretends not to…claiming that all these extras are necessary if you want to pull the crowds in, but secretly…' She shook her head and laughed. 'At Christmas he always organises a family event. I don't really know what to call it. It's a sort of play, only everyone gets involved and we all have to get dressed up and there's no audience, only every one of us hamming it up and acting out the roles Guy's given us.'

'It sounds wonderful,' Chrissie told her and meant it. Suddenly the light went out of her eyes when she realised that *her* child would never be able to take part in such festivities, that *her* child would never know the fun and pleasure that went with being part of such a large and extended family group.

As she looked round, a stall selling art deco jewellery caught her eye. It was one of her mother's passions and instinctively Chrissie began to walk towards it.

Across from the stall, a flat waggon pulled by a large shire-horse was having beer barrels unloaded from it. Chrissie heard the warning shout but didn't realise what had happened until a child screamed and she saw the heavy barrel that had broken free from the load was rolling straight towards her.

For some reason, instead of moving she discovered she could only stand there transfixed, paralysed, her heart pounding with fear, the ominous rumble of the barrel accentuated by the dull roaring she could hear in her ears.

'Chrissie!' She heard Guy's voice and turned instinctively to look for him, only to see him running through the crowd towards her, his face set with tension.

'Guy,' she whispered, then her knees suddenly started to buckle beneath her and the whole world turned dark.

Groggily Chrissie opened her eyes. She was lying on something soft and warm. Warily she turned her head. A man's jacket…a man's jacket that smelled disturbingly familiar.

'Guy…' She tried to sit up and was instantly, gently, restrained.

'It's all right…everything's all right,' she heard Guy saying quietly. 'You fainted.'

'What happened…?' Dizzily Chrissie put her hand to her head. She had a vivid memory of a child screaming and a barrel… She started to shudder and cried out, 'My baby!'

'Your baby's fine,' she heard a different voice telling her.

'This is Dr Miles,' Guy informed her, introducing the fair-haired young man kneeling on the grass beside her. They were outside the stable yard in what looked very much like a private garden, Chrissie recognised as she tried to study her surroundings—not a particularly easy task from a supine position.

'The barrel…?' she questioned fearfully. But the doctor was shaking his head firmly.

'Guy reached you before it did—fortunately,' he assured her. 'Either the shock of seeing it, or the heat, combined with your pregnancy, caused you to faint, but from what I can tell both you and your baby are perfectly well, although it might be an idea to make an appointment to see your own doctor, especially if you're going to make a habit of passing out,' he teased her.

'Where's Laura?' Chrissie asked, still not fully able to take in everything that had happened.

'She's gone to get us all a cup of tea,' the doctor told her matter-of-factly, turning away from Chrissie after warning her to take her time before she tried to sit up. 'Now I'd better take a look at that arm,' he said quietly to Guy. 'Your tetanus injections *are* up to date, I hope?'

'As luck would have it, yes, they are,' Chrissie heard Guy affirming ruefully.

Because the doctor had moved in between her and Guy, she was unable to see just exactly what was wrong with Guy's arm, but she could hear him wince and draw his breath as the doctor examined him.

'Mmm…it's quite a deep gash and it's going to need stitching,' she heard him say. 'I'll clean it up as best I can and put a dressing on it but I'd like you to pop into the out-patients' department as soon as you can so they can check it over properly and stitch it for you.'

'Easier said than done,' Guy responded, shaking his head. 'I simply can't leave here until we close the fair down for the day, which won't be until this evening. I have a moral obligation to the exhibitors to be here and a legal one to Lord Astlegh who, as you very well know, only agreed to allow us to have the fair here on the understanding that I would take personal responsibility for its good conduct.'

'Oh yes, and I'm sure he'd want you to die of gangrene rather than break your word,' Laura said sarcastically, having just returned with the tea.

'Gangrene...' Only Chrissie could hear the wobble of fear in her voice as she repeated the word under her breath.

Wearily Chrissie closed her eyes. Her head was aching and she felt very queasy, but for once not because of her pregnancy. No, this time her nausea had a rather different cause.

Guy had saved her from being hit by the runaway barrel and in doing so had sustained injuries himself.

'Look, I'm sure Jenny won't mind standing in for you so that you can go to hospital,' Laura was saying to Guy. 'You could ring her now and then I can drive you both there. 'Where is your mobile?'

'I left it at the unit,' Guy told Laura. 'I'll go and get it.'

'You're not going anywhere,' she retorted. '*I* shall go and get it. You stay here with Chrissie.'

'I'd better get back to the first-aid station,' the doctor was saying as he repacked and then closed his medical case.

Chrissie waited until they had both gone before telling Guy in a low voice, 'I haven't thanked you yet for...for what you did. That barrel...'

'I didn't do anything that any other man wouldn't have done,' Guy told her tersely. 'And if it *had* hit you, it would have been my fault. After all, *I'm* responsible for the safety aspects of the fair.'

'It was an accident,' Chrissie told him quietly, but

even though she knew it was the truth, she couldn't help shuddering as she realised what could have happened if the barrel had hit her. Instinctively she wrapped her arms protectively around her stomach, causing Guy to go even paler than he already was.

'My God, what if it…where's the doctor…are you…?' he demanded hoarsely.

'I'm fine…I'm fine, Guy.' She reached out to restrain him when she saw him turning away as though he intended to go after the young doctor and drag him back by force if necessary. 'Really,' she insisted.

'I was only thinking about what might have happened if I…if you… It's funny, isn't it? A few days ago the thought of being pregnant, of having a child, was the furthest thing from my mind. Yet now the thought of *anything* happening to the baby…' She bit her lip, unable to go on.

'Don't you think *I* feel exactly the same way?'

The harshness in Guy's voice startled her.

'It isn't the same for a man,' she denied, trying to ignore the unwary response of her emotions to his words.

'No…? That's all *you* know,' he returned bitterly, adding in a low growl, 'Just what the hell do you think it does to me, knowing that you and our child could have been hurt and that I couldn't have done a damn thing to protect the both of you?'

'But you did,' Chrissie reminded him rather breathlessly, desperately wanting to change the subject to something less emotive before he realised the effect his words were having on her.

It was completely ridiculous for her to feel so…for her to wish…for her to *want* to reach out and touch him comfortingly. After all, why should she care about his pain? Why should *she* care about *him*?

She turned her head to look at him, then froze as she saw the huge livid bruise on his forehead and the dark bloodstain on the ripped sleeve of his shirt.

The sight of Guy's blood and the knowledge that it had been spilled in saving her produced a startling combination of fear, shock, pain and, yes, even anger that he should dare risk himself when she and their baby needed him so much. It was such a strong feeling and one she hadn't ever experienced before.

Chrissie glanced at the hospital waiting-room clock. She had been given the all-clear and was now waiting for the doctor to finish stitching up Guy's wound. Laura had disappeared to chat with an old friend whom she'd caught sight of in the corridor.

The waiting-room door opened and Chrissie could feel her face starting to burn with hot colour as Guy walked in.

'Is everything...are you all right?' she asked him awkwardly.

'It seems so. They fished a couple of splinters out of my arm but they seem pretty sure there aren't any more,' he told her cheerfully. 'Chrissie,' he announced in a very different and far more serious voice whilst Chrissie tensed, wondering what he was about to say. 'Couldn't we try again...start again?' she heard Guy asking her in a husky voice. He waved his good arm in her direction and added rawly, 'Today earlier...thinking, fearing... Don't we owe it to our child, son or daughter, to at least show him we cared enough for us both to be there for him?'

'Yes, I suppose we do,' Chrissie agreed in a small voice.

'We both had the advantage of growing up with two loving parents, as part of a family,' Guy continued, pressing home his advantage. 'I'm not saying that a single parent can't do a damn fine job of raising a child but...'

'I understand what you're saying,' Chrissie breathed, trying hard to swallow the lump of emotion threatening to choke her voice with the tears she dared not let him see her shed.

'But a child...two parents who love one another...who...who respect and value one another and not...'

'I'm sorry I didn't tell you the truth about Charles,' she told him with quiet dignity. 'I should have done. I *had* intended to tell you but...' She gave a small, despairing shrug, willing herself not to give in and grab hold of the emotional lifeline he was throwing her and not just for their baby's sake, either.

This afternoon, lying on the grass listening to the doctor explaining to him that he should have his gashed arm properly attended to, she had known just how deeply and permanently she loved him, but she couldn't allow herself to be swayed by her own emotions, not when she knew... Guy loved Jenny and even if he didn't, there was still the issue of the desk.

'We *could* make it work,' Guy was telling her.

'Maybe for a while,' she agreed, then forced herself to look him in the eye as she asked him, 'But what if the baby...our baby should look like Uncle Charles? Would you still want the baby then?' she asked him painfully.

Guy had gone white.

'Would *you* love him if he looked like me?' he countered.

Chrissie closed her eyes. Of course she would...of *course* she would.

'It wouldn't work, Guy,' she told him wearily. 'There'd always be the issue of the desk between us and the fact that Charlie was my uncle and then...'

She paused and gave a small shrug. 'And I'd always know that I was just a substitute for the woman you really love and that you'd only married me for the sake of our child. I suppose as far as you're concerned, if you can't have Jenny, then anyone...'

She broke off, unable to continue as emotion threatened to silence her voice completely.

'If I can't *what*? Chrissie!' Guy started to expostulate, but the waiting-room door opened at that moment to admit Laura.

Oblivious to the tense atmosphere between them and the look of extreme irritation on Guy's face, she exclaimed, 'Good, you're both ready to leave. If you like, we can drop you off at your house on the way, Guy.'

Cursing under his breath, Guy switched on the bedside light and reached for the bottle of painkillers the doctor had given him. His arm was throbbing like the devil just as he had been warned it would, but it was not that that had woken him from his shallow sleep.

He had been dreaming about Chrissie and seeing her standing there directly in the path of that damn barrel. It had taken him three seconds of frozen disbelief before he had leaped into action.

He could feel the sweat springing up all over his body. Tiredly he pushed his hand into his hair. The bruise on his temple felt raw and painful and his head ached.

After he had carried Chrissie out of the stable yard, calling to Laura to get the medical officer and whilst he waited to hear how she was…how *she* was, and not just their baby, he had known that he really didn't care any more that she hadn't told him the truth about Charlie Platt and he didn't even damn well care about the desk, either. In fact, if he could, he'd probably very likely destroy it himself, then there would be no issue over its rightful ownership.

The only *thing* that made any kind of sense to him right now—that *mattered* to him right now—was that he loved her and that he would go on loving her for the rest of his life. Somehow or other he had to find a way of convincing her of that fact. Because he was pretty sure that she loved him. No woman could fake the reaction he had seen on her face this afternoon when she realised he had been hurt. No woman would strive so hard to hide her strong emotions the way Chrissie had done at the hospital if she *didn't* love the perpetrator of them so very deeply. And as for that comment she had made about him loving Jenny!

Tomorrow he would sort it all out. Tomorrow. Now where were those painkillers? He groaned as he reached out for the bottle and in doing so knocked over the bottle of antibiotics the doctor had also given him. Well, he certainly wasn't going to pick them up now. They could stay where they were until morning.

CHAPTER NINE

ONLY by morning Guy was in no state...no state at all to do any such thing.

By morning Guy was both unconscious and feverish, tossing uncomfortably in his bed, muttering into the silence of the room, his hair and body soaked with perspiration whilst under the dressing the hospital had put on his wound his arm had swollen to almost twice its original size and was pulsing with the pain generated by the poison that was slowly spreading in a dark red line up his arm towards his armpit.

'Hello, Jon, you look a bit frazzled,' Ruth greeted her nephew with a smile as their paths crossed in the square.

'Mmm...just a bit,' Jon agreed. 'I had to do the school run this morning because Jenny had to go to Fitzburgh Place to stand in for Guy again. He was supposed to be there at eight apparently, but he hasn't turned up and Jen couldn't raise him on the phone. Maybe they kept him in hospital overnight.'

'Hospital?' Ruth queried.

'Mmm... There was a bit of an accident at the Antiques Fair yesterday. It seems a barrel broke free from a dray and if Guy hadn't intervened, young Chrissie could have been very seriously injured.'

'Oh dear. Well, I don't think Guy *is* in hospital,' Ruth informed him. 'I certainly saw Laura dropping

him off at home yesterday. She had Chrissie in the
car with her, too. Is there a reconciliation on the cards
there, do you think?' Ruth asked her nephew.

Jon looked grave. 'It would be nice to think so
but...'

'Lovers *do* quarrel and make up,' Ruth pointed out.

'Well, yes, and if it was merely a lovers' quarrel,
I would agree with you, but there's also the side issue
of this desk—Ben's desk according to Guy, but her
family's according to Chrissie.'

'Yes, I can see what you mean,' Ruth agreed.

'Look, I'm sorry to have to dash off,' Jon apologised, bending his head to kiss her, 'but I really must
go. I've got a client due in ten minutes.'

As she watched him walk away before she had a
chance to reply, Ruth hoped that his secretary, a nice
woman, would notice that he had a piece of toast
sticking out of his jacket pocket.

It was a lovely morning, but as she retraced her
steps Ruth's mind wasn't really on the weather. It was
such a shame that something so silly as a mere desk—
not even a particularly valuable desk at that—should
be keeping two people, so plainly meant to be together as Guy and Chrissie, apart...three people if you
counted their baby and Ruth certainly did.

But unfortunately she wasn't Solomon and this
problem couldn't be solved by offering, *threatening*,
to cut the desk in two.

In two... Ruth frowned. Something had been tug-
ging irritatingly at the corner of her mind ever since
the whole issue of the desk had come up.

*   *   *

'What are you doing here?' Ben demanded tetchily when he saw Ruth.

'I thought I'd come and see how you are,' Ruth informed him, ignoring his scowl. 'Oh, and while I'm here there's something I want to check up on in the library,' she added.

'Oh, and what might that be?' Ben demanded.

'Nothing that would interest you,' Ruth informed him with deliberate vagueness. 'By the way, I've asked Mrs Brookes to bring us a tray of tea.'

'Tea. Bah…can't stand the stuff. It makes my rheumatism worse,' Ben complained grumpily.

'Really, *I've* never heard of it having that effect on anyone before,' Ruth replied straight-faced, managing not to point out that the heavy port that Ben enjoyed after his evening meal was far more likely to be the culprit.

However, she noticed that when Mrs Brookes had brought the tea, Ben seemed to enjoy his well enough, although she could tell by the way he moved that he was suffering a great deal of discomfort.

Hopefully once he had had his operation he would be able to move about more easily and he should certainly have less pain, but since she knew he hated to be reminded of it, she wisely said nothing, waiting until they had both had a second cup of tea before announcing that she would just pop into the library before she left.

She knew exactly what she was looking for. Quickly closing the door, she went immediately to the cupboard housing the meticulous account books that went back to her father's time.

It took her rather longer than she had hoped to find

what she was looking for, mainly because she hadn't known which year she needed to look under and consequently had had to search through several before finding the item or rather items she had been searching for. When she did, she couldn't help giving a small, triumphant yelp of exultation as she read the entry she had turned up.

There it was as clear as day, in her father's elegant copperplate hand.

Account...To Thomas Berry, woodcarver, £2 10s 6d. each for the construction of a pair of matching desks in yew tree wood.

Two...a pair! So she had been *right*. She *knew* there just couldn't have been one. It would have been completely out of character for her father, a perfectionist in everything he did, to go to the trouble of having the Chester family's heirloom desks copied and only having *one* made instead of the matching pair *they* possessed.

So at least she knew there *had* been two desks, which meant that both Guy and Chrissie *could be* right in claiming different ownership, but what still rather intrigued her was the matter of how one of the desks came to be in the possession of Chrissie's family in the first place.

She heard the study door rattle and was just closing the account book when Ben limped in.

'Still here?' he grumbled, then tensed as he saw what she was holding. 'What are you doing with that?' he demanded harshly.

'I was just checking something in it,' Ruth responded calmly.

'You...you had no right,' he began to bluster. 'You—'

'Ben, I'm your *sister*,' Ruth reminded him firmly. 'You can't bully or frighten me. I have *every* right. Now there's something I want to ask you...about the missing desk...or rather the two missing desks.'

She watched as he sat down very heavily.

'I don't know what you're talking about,' he declared with patent untruth.

'Oh, yes, you do,' Ruth argued cheerfully. 'You know very well what I mean. You really are naughty, Ben,' she chided him. 'You should at least have told the police that there were originally two desks.'

'No, I shouldn't.' Ben glowered at her. 'I gave my father my word it would never be mentioned...*our* secret.'

'Well, I certainly didn't make him any such promise,' Ruth told him crisply, 'and I have every intention of telling them. Good heavens, Ben, what does it matter? So there were two desks. Anyone with a logical brain can work out for themselves that there had to be, especially once Rose Oldham can prove the identity of the one the police are holding. So come on...tell me...what happened?'

Ben scowled even more deeply.

'I mean to have the truth, Ben,' Ruth warned him, 'and I'm quite prepared to stay here until I get it. Our father commissioned a pair of matching desks, copies of the ones owned by the Chester family. I know that much. At some point or other, one of the desks became the property of the Platt family. How?'

Ben frowned and shifted uncomfortably from one foot to the other before telling Ruth hesitantly, 'Father gave it to the Platt girl as a dowry...a wedding gift. She was working here as a nursemaid.'

'Our *father* gave a nursemaid one of a pair of desks he had specifically commissioned as a wedding gift?' Ruth snorted. 'I'm not saying that he was a mean man, Ben, but I *know* he would never have done anything like that...not unless he had some definite reason.'

'I don't know how she came by it,' Ben grumbled. 'Perhaps she stole it...or...'

'Ben,' Ruth warned before adding thoughtfully, 'Of course, we can always wait until Chrissie's mother arrives. She probably knows how it came into her family.'

'No, she doesn't,' Ben returned swiftly. 'The girl knew what side her bread was buttered on. And old Platt, well, he would have kept quiet about it, as well. Yes, and would most likely have taken it to the grave with him.'

'Ben...I'm sorry. I'm just not following you,' Ruth interrupted him, frowning.

'Told you plainly enough, haven't I?' Ben harrumphed. 'The nursemaid got herself in the family way and had to be married off. Old Platt had already lost one wife and there were no children, so he was glad enough to take her on, but she insisted that she deserved something and threatened to kick up such a fuss that Father was forced to let her take the desk, otherwise...'

'You mean that the nursemaid, Chrissie's great-grandmother, was pregnant with our father's child?'

Ruth demanded. 'And that *he* married her off to Archie Platt…paid her off with a *desk*?'

'It was what she wanted,' Ben defended, 'and damn lucky to get it, too, yes, and a husband.'

'A *nursemaid*, Ben,' Ruth protested. 'She wouldn't have been much more than a child…seventeen or eighteen at the most. Oh, the poor girl, and she probably loved him, I imagine.'

'Who? Archie Platt? I doubt it. He must have been twice her age and—'

'No. Father,' Ruth corrected him. 'The poor girl. So Chrissie isn't just a Platt. She's part Crighton, as well.' Ruth smiled.

'Now don't you go telling anyone that,' Ben urged. 'I gave my word.'

'I doubt it's a relationship *she* will particularly want to lay claim to herself,' Ruth informed him tartly, mentally reflecting that she could guess now where Charlie Platt had got his less attractive characteristics from. There was a certain very selfish and greedy streak that notoriously manifested itself every now and again in the male Crighton line.

Jon's twin brother, David, had it. Jon's own elder son, Max, most certainly had it. Her own father, she suspected, had had it, too, and from the sound of it, Charlie Platt had inherited it in full measure, but of course, *that* was simply a *private* opinion and could never be proved.

Chrissie and Guy would both have to be told and so would the authorities—the police. Ruth doubted that Ben would react well to this news. She frowned a little.

Whilst there was now a logical explanation for

Chrissie and Guy believing that they knew the rightful ownership of the desk, Ruth was too wise and knew too much about life to believe that this knowledge could instantly make everything right between them.

No, the reasons for them both doubting one another, for them *both* perhaps subconsciously *wanting* to doubt one another went far deeper than the issue of the desk.

Mutual fear of commitment would perhaps be the fashionable media explanation; a mutual fear of allowing themselves to truly trust another person was, in Ruth's view, closer to the truth. But then, who was she to blame them for that?

For the sake of their unborn child, she hoped their differences could be resolved, but with love rather than by necessity. A sterile relationship without trust was no relationship in which to bring up a young life, no relationship at all, but she was perhaps old-fashioned in her outlook, Ruth acknowledged, and of course, *she* had the benefit of her own mistakes, her own wrong judgements, to guide her.

CHAPTER TEN

CHRISSIE wakened abruptly, sitting up in bed, her hand on her stomach, her heart beating fast, not knowing what had brought her so immediately out of her deep sleep, only relieved to discover as she came fully awake that the anxiety that had tugged at her subconscious forcing her to wake up had nothing to do with the new life all her maternal instincts told her was perfectly comfortable and happy in its protected environment.

So what then had made her wake up feeling so fearful and anxious? Even through the curtains and as early as it was, she could see that the sun was already shining, the ambience within Laura's comfortable guest room was as relaxed and welcoming as it always was, and so far as she could tell, yesterday's unpleasant experience had left her remarkably physically unscathed. In fact, she suspected, of the two of them, that Guy...

Guy... Her heart suddenly lurched so heavily against her chest wall that she could feel the physical shock of it. By the corresponding tightness within it, the struggle she had to catch her breath and without even knowing how, she knew immediately that something was wrong with Guy, knew it so overwhelmingly and intensely that she was already out of bed, hurrying into Laura's bedroom to shake her awake.

'Chrissie...what is it, what's wrong? The baby...?'

164

Laura mumbled as she opened her eyes and saw Chrissie bending anxiously over her.

'No, not me. I'm fine,' Chrissie assured her. 'It's Guy.'

'Guy...?' Frowning, Laura started to sit up. 'Why...what...has he...?'

'I'm not sure. I can't explain it. I just *know* something is wrong,' Chrissie told her urgently. 'Laura, something *is* wrong...I know it. I...I feel it.'

'What makes you think so?' Laura asked her doubtfully, fully awake now. 'I know what happened yesterday must have given you a bad shock, and a woman in your condition...'

Her *condition*! Chrissie grimaced. In a way, Laura was right; it *was* her condition that was responsible for making her feel so concerned. But the condition making her feel so anxious, so sure that something was wrong, was not the fact that she was carrying Guy's child as Laura seemed to think, but the fact that she loved him. Her *love* for him was the condition that was giving her this feeling. This knowing...

'Laura, please,' Chrissie pleaded, glancing at the telephone beside the bed. 'Just ring him.'

'All right,' Laura agreed, 'but I doubt he's going to be very pleased at being woken up at six o'clock in the morning.'

Chrissie didn't care; she was being driven by a knowledge, an instinct, that simply couldn't be ignored.

She watched as Laura dialled Guy's number, then waited as she heard the telephone ring and ring and ring...

'He's probably so drugged by the stuff the hospital gave him that he can't hear the phone,' Laura reassured her. 'I know you're worried about him,' she told Chrissie gently as she finally replaced the receiver. 'But you heard what they said at the hospital...he's fine.'

'Laura...please...please,' Chrissie pleaded again, her voice quivering with the intensity of her emotion. 'I know there's something wrong.'

As she turned away and started to head for the door, Laura asked her tiredly, 'Where are you going?'

'I'm going to get dressed and drive round to Guy's,' Chrissie informed her determinedly.

Behind her, she could hear Laura sighing.

'All right...wait...I'll come with you,' Laura conceded, 'but I warn you now, I doubt he's going to welcome us with open arms or thank us for disturbing him.'

It was an unfamiliar sensation to be out and abroad when the day was so young and fresh. In other circumstances, Chrissie acknowledged she would have enjoyed the breathlessly clean newness of the day and the sense of being in tune with nature and the world around her, but much as it gave her pleasure to watch a pair of geese taking off from a small lake as they drove past it, that pleasure was only fleeting and marred by the dark current of her underlying concern for Guy.

'For someone who claims not to love him, you're certainly showing an awful lot of anxiety over Guy,' Laura remarked dryly as they drove into the empty streets of Haslewich.

'I...I do love him,' Chrissie admitted huskily. 'But I can't have a relationship with a man who doesn't trust or respect me and who...' She stopped abruptly, unable to go on, shaking her head slightly.

'I'm sorry, I didn't mean to upset you,' Laura apologised gently.

'You didn't,' Chrissie returned ruefully. 'I upset myself.'

'We'll have to park here,' Laura told her.

The church walk was empty and quiet as they entered it. Chrissie looked anxiously towards the house; the upstairs curtains were closed but those downstairs were open.

Laura knocked briskly on the door and then rang the bell, wincing as it pealed loudly through the house. 'Well, that should wake him,' she commented wryly, but although they waited for several minutes, there were still no sounds from within.

'Perhaps we should ring again,' Chrissie urged her, but Laura shook her head.

'I've got a better idea,' she declared firmly, rooting in her handbag and producing a small bunch of keys. She rummaged through them and, with a pleased smile, selected one.

'Guy gave me a key so that I could keep a check on things when he goes away,' she explained. 'Come on,' she instructed Chrissie briskly as she inserted it in the lock and turned the handle.

As she followed Laura, Chrissie shivered. The house felt so quiet, deathly quiet.

Laura began to climb the stairs, Chrissie close behind her. The door to Guy's bedroom was closed. Calling out his name, Laura turned the handle and went in, the somewhat irritated scepticism she had been exhibiting from the moment Chrissie had woken her up suddenly abandoned as she reached the bed and exclaimed in a shocked voice, 'Oh my God!'

'Laura, what is it...what's wrong?' Chrissie asked

anxiously as Laura's body blocked her view of the bed and of Guy.

'I'm not sure, but it looks like blood poisoning,' Laura answered faintly, moving to one side so that Chrissie could now see Guy's arm.

Even in the shadowed light of the curtained room, Chrissie could see quite plainly how swollen and inflamed the arm was. She could also see the tell-tale red line running towards his armpit.

'Guy. Guy,' Laura called, shaking her brother gently by the shoulder, but although he muttered and frowned, moving uncomfortably beneath her touch, he didn't open his eyes.

Thank God she'd followed her instincts, Chrissie fervently thought ten minutes later as a grim-faced ambulance man confirmed that Guy needed immediate hospital treatment.

Four hours of waiting while Guy went into surgery to have a sliver of wood removed had taken their toll on Chrissie, and if Laura had entertained any doubts about the strength of Chrissie's feelings for Guy, these past hours would have determinedly routed them.

If ever she had witnessed a woman deeply in love, then Chrissie was that woman, and Laura hadn't forgotten that if it hadn't been for Chrissie's insistence, Guy could have been even more seriously ill than he already was.

Outside the door of his room, Chrissie hung back, telling Laura huskily, 'You go first.'

Wisely Laura didn't argue. As she opened the door, she saw the way Guy's eyes lit up with hope and expectation, which quickly faded when he saw her.

'I hope you're up to having more than one visitor,'

she told Guy cryptically as she beckoned Chrissie into the room. This time, she noted with satisfaction, the intense emotion in Guy's eyes didn't fade as he watched Chrissie walk uncertainly towards his bed.

'How...how are you feeling?' Chrissie asked him tritely, her throat so dry with tension and the aftermath of her fear for him that she could hardly get the words out.

'Sore and apparently fortunate to be here,' he commented wryly.

'Well, you've got Chrissie to thank for the fact that you are,' Laura informed him matter-of-factly, ignoring the warning glance Chrissie was giving her. 'I must admit, when she woke me at six o'clock this morning claiming you were ill, I took an awful lot of persuading that she was right. It's just as well she's so tenacious, otherwise...'

She had her reward in the look Guy gave Chrissie as he whispered, 'You knew...but...'

'Chrissie, I really think you should sit down,' Laura insisted firmly. She turned her attention back to Guy. 'She's been pacing the waiting-room floor for the past four hours,' she explained. 'I felt exhausted just watching her, which reminds me, there's a phone call I have to make. If you two will just excuse me...'

She was gone before Chrissie could open her mouth to protest. Her heart started to thump very heavily and she turned uncertainly towards the door.

As though he sensed what she was feeling, Guy held out his good arm to her and pleaded, 'Don't go, Chrissie. Please...'

When she turned back in response, he told her quietly, 'The surgeon tells me I'm lucky to be alive. Another few hours and the septicaemia could have been so bad it would have meant amputation at best and at worst…'

The look in Chrissie's eyes and the small sound she made in her throat told him all he wanted to know.

'Oh God, Chrissie,' he said roughly. 'What have we *done* to each other? *Why* have we made such a mess of things? I can remember thinking last night just before the fever made it impossible for me to think, that if anything happened…you'd never know just how much I love you…just how much I wish this whole sorry business of that damned desk had never come between us, or how much I wish I'd never let my idiotic prejudice against your uncle—'

'Laura told me what he did to you when you were a child,' Chrissie interrupted him huskily, 'how he bullied you. He did the same to my mother even though she was much older than Charlie. She…she told me once that she used to feel so guilty because she hated him so much.'

'Yes, it must have been hard for her,' Guy agreed quietly, 'but not as hard as I've made things for you.'

Somehow or other without Chrissie being aware of how it happened, they were holding hands, their fingers entwined, their body language giving away all the things that logic and suspicion had urged them to suppress.

'You're having my baby,' Guy whispered rawly. 'When the surgeon told me how close I'd been to… I couldn't bear to think that our child would come into the world without my knowing…without my being there to share the miracle we've created between us. Without my being there to look after and protect the both of you the way… I *want* to be there, Chrissie, not just for our baby, but for you, as well.'

'I want you to be there, too,' Chrissie heard herself admitting as her tears started to fall. Guy, ignoring her protests, heaved himself up in the bed and, using his good arm, drew her down against him, gently kissing her head and trying to comfort her.

'I *know* there are still problems,' he admitted when she finally lifted her head from his chest. He smiled lovingly down at her and smoothed her damp hair back off her face. 'But somehow we'll find a way to work them out.'

'I never meant to keep the truth from you,' Chrissie murmured sadly.

'Shush,' Guy ordered her firmly and she gave him a painful smile. 'It wasn't so much the fact that you were Charlie's niece that bothered me,' Guy explained. 'It was knowing that you didn't trust me enough to tell me...and that hurt. Stupidly because I was hurt...I lashed out unforgivably. Instead of admitting that I *was* hurt and behaving like an adult, I reacted like a child, accusing and blaming you.'

'The reason I didn't tell you was because I loved you too much,' Chrissie responded shakily. 'I was too afraid of losing you and then my mother suggested that I should keep quiet about being related to Charlie and I knew how you felt about him...' She shook her head, then went on quietly, 'I was hurt, too, you know, when you weren't honest with me about your...your relationship with Jenny.'

She paused and waited painfully to see how he would respond.

'Yes,' Guy agreed after a small pause. 'I wasn't entirely honest with you about that, I know—'

'Because you didn't want me to know how much you loved her,' Chrissie interjected sadly.

'No!' Guy denied her assertion so forcefully that he winced as he tried to catch hold of her and jarred his bandaged arm.

'No,' he reiterated more gently whilst Chrissie fussed over his pain. 'No, the reason I didn't tell you about her was because I was ashamed of myself for...for being weak enough at that particular time in my life to believe that the answer to all my problems lay in forming a relationship with another man's wife, a woman who I already knew in my heart of hearts was quite simply not available to me. I was at an age where I *wanted* to fall in love, to settle down and have a family, but because it wasn't happening, because there was no one around who appealed to me in that way, I convinced myself that I was in love with Jenny, a woman who already had her family and who was so much in love with her own husband that there was absolutely no possibility of her ever falling in love with me.

'I never really loved Jenny at all, Chrissie, and she was wise enough to know as much and that was why I was so reluctant to discuss what happened with you. I didn't want to expose myself to you as a flawed human being. The truth is that I didn't have a clue what real love was until I met you...until I saw you, and then when I had, when I did, the truth was so illuminating, so blinding, that...' He paused and shook his head. 'I'm very fond of Jenny and I always will be, but *you* are the woman I love. You will *always* be the woman I love.'

'Even though you think I'm lying about the desk?' Chrissie asked him quietly.

Guy sighed. 'I don't know what to say. I only know the evidence of my eyes.'

'I understand,' Chrissie agreed quietly, disentangling herself from his embrace and walking slowly towards the door.

She was just about to open it when she heard Guy calling her name. Thinking that something was wrong with his arm, she reacted instinctively, turning round and running back to his side.

'Guy, what is it?' she demanded. 'What's wrong… your arm…?'

'My arm's fine,' he replied in a muffled voice. 'But I'm not. Oh God, Chrissie, I don't give a damn about the wretched desk. You're what matters to me…all that matters to me. I can sell my share in the business, we can move, go and make a fresh start somewhere where no one…'

Chrissie stared at him. 'You'd do *that* for me?' she whispered. 'Even though…'

'I'd do *anything* for you,' Guy groaned as he reached for her, pulling her down onto the bed beside him.

'Anything and *everything*. I *love* you, Chrissie, and that's *all* **that** matters, and just as soon as I get out of this damned hospital, you and I are going to sit down together and make plans…not just for our own future but for our child's, as well,' he promised her firmly as he started to kiss her.

Laura opened the door, saw the couple on the bed, Guy's good arm locking Chrissie to him as he kissed her, and discreetly closed the door again.

'We're going to be so happy together, the three of us,' Guy declared when he finally released her, but although she smiled at him, Chrissie wondered.

It was all very well for Guy to talk of leaving Haslewich and making a new start, but the issue of her family's trustworthiness would always be there between them, no matter how deeply they tried to bury it.

'We've had an official invitation to go round and have tea with Ruth Reynolds, one of my neighbours,' Guy announced as Chrissie walked into his sitting room.

He had been allowed home from the hospital the previous day but only with the proviso that there was someone to look after him.

There was no way *she* could take on the task, Laura had insisted determinedly. Not with her own husband due home in the next twenty-four hours, and the horses to look after, so of course Chrissie had really no option other than to take on the role in her stead.

'Oh, when does she want us to go?' Chrissie asked him.

'Come in, both of you,' Ruth invited warmly as she answered the door to Guy and Chrissie's ring. 'I've invited Jon to join us,' she added unexpectedly as she led the way to her pretty drawing room. 'I feel it's important that he should be here, if only as an informal recorder and, of course, to give corroboration to what I have to say, just in case. But I'm rather jumping the gun. How are you feeling, Guy?' she enquired solicitously.

'Much better than I was,' Guy told her wryly. 'Much better than I might have been if it hadn't been for Chrissie,' he added as he turned towards her and smiled tenderly.

Ruth had, of course, heard about their reconciliation, and as Jenny had said, it was lovely to hear that they had resolved their differences and that their love for one another had proved to be strong enough to overcome them.

'I'm so glad for them both,' Jenny had continued. 'They are so obviously right for one another.'

'Come in and sit down,' Ruth invited. 'Chrissie, if you wouldn't mind pouring the tea, I have a rather interesting story to tell you both.'

She smiled at Chrissie's slightly surprised look as the younger woman dutifully went over to the table and started to pour the tea.

'I've been rather puzzled and concerned,' Ruth began, 'about this problem concerning the true ownership of the desk that was found in Charlie Platt's house. So I've been doing a little bit of investigating. As Jon is aware, my father had rather a thing about his relatives in Chester, and since he knew that the desk he had copied was one of a pair made as birthday gifts for twin daughters in the Chester family, it seemed to me that it didn't make sense that he should only have had the *one* desk made. That's why I decided to do some research....'

She paused before reaching for the heavy book that lay on the floor at her feet.

'This is the account book for the year when the desk was commissioned, or should I say when the *desks* were commissioned?'

It took some time for her wry words to sink in, but once they had, Guy exclaimed, 'You mean there were *two* desks, but—'

'Yes, there were two desks,' Ruth interjected calmly. 'Two identical desks, just like the pair made for the Chester family.'

'But that still doesn't explain how one of them

came into the possession of my family,' Chrissie observed.

'That it doesn't,' Ruth agreed quietly. 'Accounts are simply statements of funds paid out and gathered in.'

'Surely my great-grandfather didn't *buy* one of the desks?' Chrissie questioned doubtfully. 'That would—'

'No, Chrissie, he didn't,' Ruth returned gently before looking at Jon. 'Our father, Ben's and mine, was married twice. Our mother died shortly after my birth and a young girl was hired to help out in the nursery.' Ruth paused and then continued.

'That girl was your great-grandmother, Chrissie. A relationship developed between her and my father, and when she became pregnant he apparently persuaded her to marry one of his tenant farmers, who was himself a widower with no children.

'It was agreed between the two men that the baby, a son, would be brought up as the farmer's child. He, it seems, was already middle-aged and desperate for an heir. A sum of money also changed hands.' Ruth grimaced slightly. 'That poor girl. I suspect she must have loved my father very much, so much so it seems that she pleaded with him to be allowed to take with her to her new home some memento of what they had shared. He agreed and she chose the desk,' Ruth concluded simply.

Chrissie stared at her in shock before demanding huskily, 'Is this really true? It seems so…'

'Yes, it's really true, Chrissie,' Jon confirmed with quiet authority.

'But *why* hasn't my mother ever said? Why…?'

'I doubt very much that she knew,' Ruth told her.

'I certainly knew nothing about it myself and Ben, my brother, only found out when our father was dying. According to Ben, it was confided to him as a secret that he was sworn to keep. It was only when I challenged him about the fact that there were two desks and threatened to inform the police that he finally admitted the truth to me.'

'I still can't quite take it all in,' Chrissie whispered, tears filling her eyes as she turned to Ruth and confided emotionally, 'You can't know how much I've been dreading having my mother identify the desk. How much…'

'I think I can,' Ruth corrected her gently.

Guy still hadn't said anything, but his expression gave him away. 'Two desks,' he announced grimly, standing up now and pacing the floor. 'Of course. *Why* didn't *I* guess that for myself? I *knew* there were two originals.'

'There was really no reason why you should have done,' Ruth soothed him. 'You had, after all, only seen the one and no one had ever suggested to you that there might originally have been two.'

'Maybe not, but I should have thought…*questioned*… Chrissie!'

'It's all right,' Chrissie reassured him unsteadily as she reached for his hand. 'Ruth's right. You really couldn't have known and,' she added with heartwarming honesty, 'in your shoes, I would probably have reacted just as you did.'

The look Guy gave her made Ruth bite her lip and look away. Some feelings, some emotions, were just too intense, too passionate, too raw, to be witnessed by any outsiders.

'You're a liar,' she heard Guy saying huskily, 'and a very generous one.'

Chrissie shook her head. She was still feeling too overwhelmed by Ruth's astonishing revelations. 'I can't believe this is happening,' she told Ruth and Jon shakily. 'It seems so...well, it's so unexpected.'

'Well, it certainly helps to explain where Charlie got his rogue genes from,' Ruth commented humorously, explaining wryly to Chrissie, 'Unfortunately there is a certain inherited characteristic in the Crighton ancestry that tends to produce the odd individual who is not only monumentally selfish, but totally lacking in what the rest of us might describe as moral responsibility, as well, which reminds me...'

She stood up, then walked over to Chrissie and embraced her warmly.

'Welcome to the Crighton family, my dear.'

The *Crighton* family. Chrissie opened her mouth and then closed it again.

'It's all right,' Ruth told her in a kind voice. 'We'll all understand if you choose not to acknowledge us as part of your family.'

'I just don't know what my mother is going to say about all this,' Chrissie exclaimed weakly.

'I expect you and Guy would like some time on your own now to talk over...everything,' Ruth said, gently touching Chrissie lightly on the wrist and then giving her another warm hug as Chrissie stood up to leave.

Jon, too, hugged her before she left, and as she said afterwards to Guy when they were on their own in his home, 'They were both just so warm and welcoming.' She started to cry and Guy who had been getting them both a drink walked across the kitchen to catch hold of her and demanded gruffly, 'What is it…what's wrong?'

'Nothing,' Chrissie hiccupped into his shoulder. 'I'm just so glad that it's all over. I was so afraid that this would always haunt us, that it would always come between us…that you'd never be able to completely trust me.'

'*Me* trust *you*?' As he bent his head to kiss her, the apology he was starting to make was muffled by the warm pressure of Chrissie's mouth against his, soothing the pain of his guilt and remorse. 'First thing tomorrow morning we're flying to Amsterdam,' Guy informed her huskily once she had released his mouth, 'and it won't just be an engagement ring I shall be buying you. And while we're there we might as well add an eternity ring, as well,' he added, as he gently stroked her finger, 'because this time, my love, it is for eternity.'

'Yes, it is,' Chrissie concurred softly.

'May I see your rings? Oh yes, they are beautiful,' Ruth's granddaughter, Bobbie, admired as Chrissie ignored the shower of rose petals one of the wedding guests was throwing over both her and Guy to step forward and extend her hand.

Chrissie had surprised herself by choosing not an antique ring as she had first intended, but a modern trio of rings, especially designed for her by one of Amsterdam's top jewellers. The heart-shaped diamond of her engagement ring had been chosen by Guy, and Chrissie had gasped over its breathtaking magnificence.

It only stopped short of being vulgar by just a heartbeat, she had told him at the time, but both the jew-

eller and Guy had argued and assured her that in com-
parison with some of the solitaires they sold, it was,
in fact, rather modest. The simple band it was set into
had been specially made to interlink with both the
diamond-studded, entwined-rope design of her white-
and-gold wedding and eternity rings, whilst around
the centre of the eternity ring ran an additional ring
of perfect but more modestly sized individual dia-
monds.

'They all interlock and belong together, like the
three of us,' Guy had told Chrissie tenderly when they
had chosen the design. The three of them.

Her wedding outfit had been made in Chester, its
simple cut and the richness of the heavy cream satin
discreetly masking her growing pregnancy. That was
why Chrissie had decided against a traditional wedding gown and opted instead for a full-length plainly
cut dress and a matching full-length satin coat over it
with a small train at the back.

'I'm not ashamed of the fact that I'm carrying our
child,' she had told her mother proudly. 'But we *are*
having a church wedding and I just don't feel that a
traditional dress would be appropriate.'

'You'll look lovely, darling,' her mother had assured her as they studied the design Chrissie had chosen.

And of course she did.

More than lovely as Guy had already told her.

She smiled at him now, touching his arm to draw
his attention to where her mother was standing with
his sister, Laura, the two of them deep in conversation.

The fact that Laura and her mother had struck up
such an immediate bond had been an additional bonus

so far as Chrissie was concerned. It had been Laura who had taken charge when her parents had travelled south, insisting that they stay with her and her husband and very firmly dealing with her mother's reservations about how she might be judged.

'You are *not* your brother. You are yourself and people will judge you accordingly,' Laura had told her forthrightly.

And so it had proved to be. Several women who had been at school with her mother had made very warm overtures to her. Chrissie might suspect that Laura had had a hand in their warm welcome, but she certainly wasn't going to spoil her mother's pleasure in being remembered by saying so. And both Guy's family and the Crightons, as well, had made it plain that they considered them very welcome additions to their family circles.

Only Natalie had held herself rather aloof, and Chrissie hadn't been upset at all to learn that she had decided to move to London.

Her mother had received the news about their connection with the Crightons with the same astonishment as Chrissie, but what had touched Chrissie most of all was to overhear her mother remarking to Jenny the day before the wedding that she and Chrissie's father were definitely thinking of moving South when they retired.

'After all,' she had said to Jenny, 'it won't just be our daughter and son-in-law who are living here, but our grandchildren, as well.'

'If I didn't know better,' Guy teased her as they watched one of his teenage nieces flirting outrageously with a gangly-looking boy who seemed more embarrassed than flattered by her attention, 'I almost suspect that you'd rather stay here than go to Barbados with me.'

'Only almost?' Chrissie teased him back. 'It's so wonderful to be part of a big family, Guy, to know that our child, our children, will be growing up with that advantage, but it's nowhere near as wonderful as knowing you love me,' she whispered huskily in his ear. 'And as for Barbados...'

'Barbados. Why the hell didn't I just book us a suite at the Grosvenor in Chester?' Guy groaned against her mouth as he bent his head to kiss her. 'Do you know how long that flight is?'

'We've still got the reception to get through yet,' Chrissie reminded him demurely.

'Just you wait until I get you on my own,' Guy warned her.

'On my own?' Chrissie raised an eyebrow and patted her gently rounding body teasingly. 'I don't think so,' she reminded him archly. 'By the way, I'm glad they've caught the gang responsible for those break-ins.'

'So am I,' Guy agreed, giving her a sombre look. 'I can't believe that I even thought in my dreams that you were remotely involved.'

'Shush.' Chrissie placed her fingers over his lips. 'It did all seem to fit into place and the gang did have a female member.'

'I don't deserve you,' Guy whispered tenderly.

Across the churchyard, Madeleine Crighton saw them laughing and witnessed the look they exchanged, the love they so obviously shared so palpable you could almost reach out and touch it.

Tiredly she looked away.

When she had been pregnant with both their children, Max had treated her not with tenderness and love but with acidic fury, reminding her that he had not wanted children, just as he had not really wanted her.

She started to make her way quickly through the crowd to where Jenny, Max's mother, was standing with the children.

Thinking about Max and their marriage was something Maddy tried very hard not to do these days. Their marriage... What marriage? It was simply a worthless piece of paper, a legal document. Max didn't love her and she was beginning to question if he had ever loved her. He made her feel so worthless, so useless. In his eyes she felt unwanted, undesirable, and she was almost glad of the physical distance between them, the 'business' that had taken him to Spain.

Almost... A part of her still remembered how it had once been...how they had once been...just...

'Mmm...this is pure heaven,' Guy exclaimed contentedly as they lay on the bed of their holiday villa, the fan whirring soporifically above them as it cooled the hot Barbadian night air.

'Was it worth waiting for?' Chrissie teased him tongue-in-cheek as he raised himself up on one elbow. He leaned over her, tracing the shape of her mouth with one fingertip, then lazily bending his head to kiss her naked breast.

'Oh, well worth waiting for,' Guy purred with the sheer satisfaction of a sensually satiated male animal.

And he was very much a male animal, Chrissie acknowledged as she watched him leave their bed and walk across the bedroom, his naked body gleaming in the soft, shadowy light. The combined warmth of the air and the heat of their passionately intense love-making had left a fine oiled sheen on his skin high-lighting its taut muscle structure. A feeling she was fast coming to recognise began stirring wantonly deep within her body.

'We never had time for this earlier,' Guy announced as he picked up the bottle of champagne. It was still in its ice bucket and he'd intended to share it before he took Chrissie to bed and they consummated physically the vows they had made verbally and emotionally to one another earlier.

Chrissie watched as he opened the bottle and poured them both a glass. She could watch him for ever, she decided contentedly. He had such masculine grace, such unconscious male arrogance and authority. He turned his head and saw her looking at him and she watched his eyes darken as he subjected her naked body to a far less inhibited and smoulderingly sensuous scrutiny than she had been giving him.

So much so that she could actually feel the colour starting to rise up under her skin. But she was pleased to note she was not the only one to be affected by the small exchange, because Guy's hand trembled slightly as he came back to the bed and handed her a brimming glass of champagne. A few drops of the golden liquid splashed onto her naked body but as she moved to wipe them away, Guy stopped her, caught hold of her free hand and then bent his head to lick away the champagne, his tongue tip doing impossibly erotic things to her nervous system as he teasingly inched closer and closer to her now very erect nipples.

'Mmm...' he murmured pleasurably, then put his

glass down, cupped the side of her breast and started to gently suck on the tight nub of flesh he had been tormenting.

Chrissie could feel the excitement pulsing through her body as she tried to stifle her soft groan of pleasure, but Guy had obviously heard it because his caresses became more intense, more purposeful, and no longer merely playful.

She wanted him…oh, how she wanted him, but he deserved a little bit of punishment himself for the way he had teased her, Chrissie decided, laughter sparkling in her eyes as she deliberately tipped some of her champagne onto his body.

'What the…' Guy exclaimed, momentarily releasing her whilst she calmly put down her glass.

Firmly pushing him onto the bed, Chrissie informed him firmly, 'If you can't take the heat, then stay out of the kitchen,' before bending her own head and slowly and deliberately following the trickle of golden liquid arrowing its way along the valley that conveniently provided a pathway down the centre of his body, lazily lapping at it with her tongue whilst at the same time deliberately encouraging it to run faster and farther.

It gave her immense satisfaction to hear Guy groaning in much the same way as she had done herself as she forced him to endure her teasing love play. Later she decided that it was the leisurely lap of honour with which she had triumphantly circled his navel, first with tiny kisses and then with the moist tip of her tongue, which had been her undoing, because it was after that and whilst she was in pursuit of the errant drop of champagne still making its way down his body that she lost control of the game. Not that she minded. Who cared about victory when being defeated, overwhelmed, by their mutual passion and then mutual love could be so hotly and sweetly satisfactory?

Dawn was just beginning to pearl the sky with its translucent light when Guy finally drew Chrissie down against his body and groaned, 'Just think... another three weeks of this. How on earth will we stand it?'

Both of them were still smiling when they finally fell asleep.

*   *   *   *   *

There will be more to come from the Crighton family in future books from Penny Jordan.

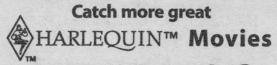 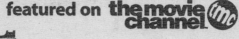

 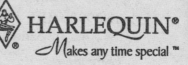

MEN at WORK

All work and no play? Not these men!

April 1998

KNIGHT SPARKS by Mary Lynn Baxter

Sexy lawman Rance Knight made a career of arresting the bad guys. Somehow, though, he thought policewoman Carly Mitchum was framed. Once they'd uncovered the truth, could Rance let Carly go...or would he make a citizen's arrest?

MEN IN UNIFORM

May 1998

HOODWINKED by Diana Palmer

CEO Jake Edwards donned coveralls and went undercover as a mechanic to find the saboteur in his company. Nothing— or no one—would distract him, not even beautiful secretary Maureen Harris. Jake had to catch the thief—*and* the woman who'd stolen his heart!

MEN OF STEEL

June 1998

DEFYING GRAVITY by Rachel Lee

Tim O'Shaughnessy and his business partner, Liz Pennington, had always been close—but never *this* close. As the danger of their assignment escalated, so did their passion. When the job was over, could they ever go back to business as usual?

TALL, DARK AND SMART

MEN AT WORK™

Available at your favorite retail outlet!

HARLEQUIN®   Silhouette®

Coming Next Month

#1959 SINFUL PLEASURES Anne Mather
Megan was back in San Felipe to find that much had changed.
Her stepsister's son, Remy, had been nine to her fifteen when
she saw him last—now he was a deeply attractive man. And
Megan sensed danger.

#1960 THE MARRIAGE CAMPAIGN Helen Bianchin
Dominic wanted Francesca, and he'd planned a very special
campaign for winning her. She may be wary of loving again,
but he was going to pursue, charm and seduce her
relentlessly—until she said yes!

#1961 THE SECRET WIFE Lynne Graham
Nothing could have prepared Rosie for Greek tycoon
Constantine Voulos—or his insistence that she marry him! But
she soon realized she couldn't just be his temporary wife. Her
secret would have to be told!

#1962 THE DIVORCÉE SAID YES! Sandra Marton
(The Wedding of the Year)
When Chase suggested to ex-wife, Annie, that they pretend to
get back together to reassure their daughter that love could
last, Annie was amazed. But then she found herself agreeing
to his plan....

#1963 ULTIMATE TEMPTATION Sara Craven
(Nanny Wanted!)
Count Giulio Falcone needed a nanny to look after his sister's
children. Lucy was in his debt *and* in his house. Suddenly she
found herself in the wrong place at the wrong time, with the
ultimate temptation—Giulio!

#1964 GIRL TROUBLE Sandra Field
(Man Talk)
Cade loved Lori, but she had two daughters—one of whom
had taken an instant dislike to him. He only wanted one
blonde in his life, not three. Trouble was, getting Lori into his
bed meant accepting the little girls into his heart!